Acting Edition

I0600465

Ken Ludwig's

The Game's Afoot; or Holmes for the Holidays

‖SAMUEL FRENCH‖

ISBN 978-0-573-70046-0

www.concordtheatricals.com
www.concordtheatricals.co.uk

FOR PRODUCTION INQUIRIES

UNITED STATES AND CANADA
info@concordtheatricals.com
1-866-979-0447

UNITED KINGDOM AND EUROPE
licensing@concordtheatricals.co.uk
020-7054-7298

Each title is subject to availability from Concord Theatricals Corp., depending upon country of performance. Please be aware that *KEN LUDWIG'S THE GAME'S AFOOT; OR HOLMES FOR THE HOLIDAYS* may not be licensed by Concord Theatricals Corp. in your territory. Professional and amateur producers should contact the nearest Concord Theatricals Corp. office or licensing partner to verify availability.

This work is published by Samuel French, an imprint of Concord Theatricals Corp.

No one shall make any changes in this title(s) for the purpose of production. No part of this book may be reproduced, stored in a retrieval system, scanned, uploaded, or transmitted in any form, by any means, now known or yet to be invented, including mechanical, electronic, digital, photocopying, recording, videotaping, or otherwise, without the prior written permission of the publisher. No one shall share this title(s), or any part of this title(s), through any social media or file hosting websites.

For all inquiries regarding motion picture, television, online/digital and other media rights, please contact Concord Theatricals Corp.

MUSIC AND THIRD-PARTY MATERIALS USE NOTE

Licensees are solely responsible for obtaining formal written permission from copyright owners to use copyrighted music and/or other copyrighted third-party materials (e.g. artworks, logos) in the performance of this play and are strongly cautioned to do so. If no such permission is obtained by the licensee, then the licensee must use only original music and materials that the licensee owns and controls. Licensees are solely responsible and liable for clearances of all third-party copyrighted materials, including without limitation music, and shall indemnify the copyright owners of the play(s) and their licensing agent, Concord Theatricals Corp., against any costs, expenses, losses and liabilities arising from the use of such copyrighted third-party materials by licensees. For music, please contact the appropriate music licensing authority in your territory for the rights to any incidental music.

IMPORTANT BILLING AND CREDIT REQUIREMENTS

If you have obtained performance rights to this title, please refer to your licensing agreement for important billing and credit requirements.

KEN LUDWIG'S THE GAME'S AFOOT; OR HOLMES FOR THE HOLIDAYS was first presented by Cleveland Play House at the Allen Theatre in Cleveland, Ohio, opening on December 2, 2011, under Artistic Director Michael Bloom, featuring scenic design by Daniel Conway, lighting design by Thom Weaver, sound design by James C. Swonger, costume design by Linda Roethke, stage management by Shannon Habenicht, and technical direction by Erik Seidel. The director was Aaron Posner. The cast was as follows:

WILLIAM GILLETTE	Donald Sage Mackay
MARTHA GILLETTE	Patricia Kilgarriff
FELIX GEISEL	Eric Hissom
MADGE GEISEL	Lise Bruneau
SIMON BRIGHT	Rob McClure
AGGIE WHEELER	Mattie Hawkinson
INSPECTOR GORING	Sarah Day
DARIA CHASE	Erika Rolfsrud

THE GAME'S AFOOT won the Edgar Allen Poe Award (the "Edgar"), awarded by the Mystery Writers of America, as the Best Mystery Play of 2012.

WHY DO MYSTERIES GRAB US?

About four years ago our family went on vacation in England, and during the London portion of the trip we went to the theatre and saw *The Mousetrap* by Agatha Christie. As you may know, *The Mousetrap* is the longest-running play in history. When we saw it, it had been running for fifty-six years (be still my heart) and it's still running today as I write this.

As I watched the play unfold that night and saw the joy that it gave to our entire family, I resolved to try and write a mystery of my own. However, I knew even then that I wouldn't have a chance of writing a good one until I figured out the allure of mysteries on the stage, and how and why the great ones entertain us so powerfully.

I started by reading every good mystery play I could lay my hands on. (Note: the phrase "mystery play" can also refer to the succession of religious plays written from the 10th to the 16th century, illustrating Bible stories and performed by craft guilds. However, these rarely involved strychnine in the soup or eccentric lady detectives in pork pie hats and are not the mysteries referred to in this essay.) What I learned from all my reading is that the greatest mystery plays written in the past hundred years have certain elements in common, and by recognizing these elements, I was able to understand more deeply the genre I was trying to tackle. Here is a summary of some of the lessons I learned from my foray into the literature of mysteries.

1. The greatest mystery plays are plotted meticulously. They're not character studies of a freewheeling nature; that's not their territory. Think of the three great Agatha Christie stage mysteries, *The Mousetrap, Witness for the Prosecution,* and *...And Then There Were None.* Each one is an absolute model of architectural plotting.

When we speak of plot, it's worth remembering the definition of plot offered by E.M. Forster in his book *Aspects of the Novel.* He illustrates the difference between story and plot as follows:

> *"The king died and then the queen died" is a story. "The king died and then the queen died of grief" is a plot. The time sequence is preserved, but the sense of causality overshadows it. Or again: "The queen died, no one knew why, until it was discovered that it was through grief at the death of the king." This is a plot with a mystery in it, a form capable of high development.*

In other words, a plot requires causality. It's not just "and then and then and then." Great thrillers sometimes take this form, but not great mysteries. In a mystery one event must lead logically to the next. Events are caused by other events. A mystery play that lacks a good plot in this sense – that is not well plotted architecturally – is never a very good one.

I recently came across a long-lost essay written in the 1930s by Agatha Christie herself, reprinted in the English publication *The*

Guardian Review. In it Christie confirms the need for tight architectural plotting in a mystery. She says, "I think the austerity and stern discipline that goes to making a 'tight' detective plot is good for one's thought processes. It is the kind of writing that does not permit loose or slipshod thinking. It all has to dovetail, to fit in as part of a carefully constructed whole."

2. The plots of great mystery plays are relentlessly linear. Mysteries take us on a ride, starting at the beginning and driving straight through to the end. Like roller coasters, the best mysteries may twist and turn, climb and plunge, but they're always headed straight forward and zoom on to the finish.

Because the best mystery plays are so linear, there is rarely time for subplots. Everything usually stays on track and contributes to the main story. Think of *Deathtrap* by Ira Levin. This story about a writer of mystery plays who plans and executes a real murder, grabs us from the first minute and never lets go. Interestingly, it's not really a whodunit so much as a whydunit – at least for the first half.

Equally compelling in the same way is *Sleuth* by Anthony Shaffer, about a man revenging his wife's infidelity: I've seen this one described as a whodunwhat – which reminds us that mysteries don't need to be formulaic, as they're sometimes described. On the contrary, originality thrives in the world of mystery, be it in the basic plot, the setting of the story, the point of view, and certainly in the final twist.

Still, the one thing the best mystery plays have in common is that there are no superfluous subplots, even for purposes of theme. Great mysteries drive straight forward, staying on track from beginning to end.

Of course mysteries sometimes contain red herrings: developments that make us believe that someone other than the culprit committed the crime. And in the best mysteries, the red herrings are woven into the forward motion of the play. There are loads of red herrings, for example, in *The Mousetrap*. Indeed, they make up the bulk of the play. The play begins by telling us that a gruesome murder was recently committed, thus laying out the exposition. It then spends most of the rest of the time introducing us to suspect after suspect until the real killer is finally revealed. Christie uses the same technique in her mystery novel *Murder on the Orient Express*. And in both cases she adds a terrific unforeseen twist at the end.

When I started to write my own mystery play, *The Game's Afoot; or Holmes for the Holidays,* I came up with a mantra for myself based on all my prior mystery reading. Just as President Clinton put a note above his desk that said, "It's the economy, stupid," I put a note above my own desk that said, "Relentlessly Entertaining." I decided that the best way to write a mystery for the stage was to make the piece as relentlessly entertaining as I possibly could – another way of saying that the forward propulsion of the piece should never flag.

3. The greatest mystery plays, like the greatest plays of any kind, somehow, almost magically, have resonances to other, deeper layers of meaning. Take the greatest mystery play ever written, *Hamlet*. It begins with the line "Who's there?" and it spends the rest of the night exploring that question. Who's there? Who am I? Who is the ghost? Who is Claudius? And in the midst of these questions, it manages to be (if it's possible to see it objectively any more) an edge-of-the-seat mystery-thriller where the victim's son tries to figure out whether to trust a ghost who tells him to kill his own uncle in revenge for the brutal murder of his father.

As *Hamlet* above all others reminds us, mysteries speak to something central to us all. We try to find out who the killer is just the way we ask other, deeper questions of identity. We want answers to vital questions that can make the world more rational and sensible because answers give us peace of mind.

4. Mysteries by their very nature contain certain recurring themes. These usually include questions about death, about justice, and about appearance versus reality. Let's start with death: Has there ever been a really successful stage mystery that doesn't have a dead body in it? If there has been, I don't know of it. In some stage mysteries, the death is far in the past – think of *Angel Street* (retitled *Gaslight* for the movies) by Patrick Hamilton, in which the murder occurred years before the opening of the play. By contrast, in *Dial M for Murder*, the murder doesn't occur until well into the second scene of the play. Similarly, in *Sleuth* and *Deathtrap*, the first half of the play is spent plotting the malefaction. But whether the death is remote or recent, onstage or off, death of some kind usually plays a part.

Sometimes the death is morally ambiguous, which raises questions about justice. Should the culprit be punished if the victim is a predator on the community? *Hamlet* raises this question squarely. Is Hamlet morally wrong for murdering Claudius if Claudius in fact murdered Hamlet's father in cold blood?

I raise this question myself in *The Game's Afoot; or Holmes for the Holidays*. It's hardly the central question of the play, but I've spoken with audience members who find the issue of justice to be one of the most interesting parts of the whole proceeding. If the culprit who is finally identified killed a character who was hateful to the whole society, is that culprit blameworthy or worthy of praise? And should that kind of culprit be punished, either by society or by the law? The answers to these questions are never clear-cut, nor should they be. But it's interesting to remember that we certainly root for Prince Hamlet every step of the way.

What about appearance versus reality? In one sense, all drama almost automatically raises this dichotomy. Actors play characters in the play; and while we're meant to be invested in the characters who embody the story, we also realize that we're sitting in a darkened room watching actors who have been hired to play parts. What is the appearance and what is the reality?

Mystery plays always take this question one step further. Many of the characters, and certainly the culprit, are disguising their true identities for the sake of some kind of escape, be it from real life or from the hangman. Disguise is central to mysteries, just as it's central to our own lives. Do we want anyone to know who we really are? How do we hide our true identities? What happens when our true identities are revealed? These questions are central to all stage mysteries, from *Hamlet* to *The 39 Steps*. And this is one of the reasons that we find mysteries so endlessly fascinating: Mysteries are journeys trying to answer the question of who we really are.

5. Finally, what we're really seeking when we look for answers in a mystery is a sense of order. In *The Game's Afoot; or Holmes for the Holidays*, I have the inspector in the play, Inspector Goring, say to the protagonist, William Gillette (the actor who played Sherlock Holmes on stage for over thirty years): "Order from chaos. Order from chaos. It's what I do."

And that's what mysteries do. They fit the pieces together. First, all the disparate elements of the story are thrown up in the air by the murder or other corrupting event. Then, miraculously, all those elements fall back to earth and fit together again, like the piece of a jigsaw puzzle, into a social order that society recognizes and approves.

We as humans seem to crave that sense of order. We find it satisfying and it gives us peace. It seems to me that it's somehow related to the puzzles that many of us like to solve on a day-to-day basis, like crosswords and Sudokus. Solving those puzzles and filling in all the space in an orderly manner gives us a sense of reassurance and closure.

Every mystery play I can think of – from the earliest examples of the genre, like *Sherlock Holmes* by William Gillette, which premiered in 1899, to more recent examples, like *The 39 Steps* by Patrick Barlow, which premiered in 2005 – has an ending where good triumphs over evil and society rights itself after a period of discord. In a sense, that's the very definition of a mystery. Order from chaos. It's what they do.

Ken Ludwig
October 2012

ABOUT THE PLAYWRIGHT

KEN LUDWIG is an internationally acclaimed playwright who has had six shows on Broadway and six in the West End. He has received two Laurence Olivier Awards (England's highest theatre honor), three Tony Award nominations, two Helen Hayes Awards, and his work has been commissioned by The Royal Shakespeare Company. *The Game's Afoot; or Holmes for the Holidays* won the Edgar Alan Poe Award for Best Mystery of 2012. *Crazy For You* won the Olivier and Tony Awards as Best Musical and *Lend Me A Tenor* (two Tony Awards and the Olivier nomination for Comedy of the Year), was called "one of the two great farces by a living writer" by *The New York Times*. Other Broadway and West End shows include *Twentieth Century* starring Alec Baldwin and Anne Heche, *Moon Over Buffalo* starring Carol Burnett, Lynn Redgrave, Joan Collins and Frank Langella, *The Adventures of Tom Sawyer*, and *Treasure Island* (Theatre Royal, Haymarket; AATE Distinguished Play Award). *Shakespeare in Hollywood* was commissioned by The Royal Shakespeare Company and won the Helen Hayes Award as Best Play. Other plays and musicals include *Leading Ladies, Be My Baby, The Beaux' Stratagem* (adaptation with Thornton Wilder at the request of the Wilder Estate), *The Three Musketeers* (Bristol Old Vic), *An American in Paris, The Fox on the Fairway, Midsummer/Jersey, 'Twas the Night Before Christmas* and *Baskerville*. He was given the 2013 Distinguished Career Award by the Southeastern Theatre Conference, the largest gathering of theatre professionals, faculty, and students in America. His work has appeared in *The Yale Review* and he has written a book for Crown Publishing entitled *How To Teach Your Children Shakespeare*. He studied music at Harvard with Leonard Bernstein and theatre history at Cambridge University, and he is on the Board of Governors of the Folder Shakespeare Library in Washington, D.C.

For more information please visit www.kenludwig.com.

CHARACTERS

WILLIAM GILLETTE
MARTHA GILLETTE
FELIX GEISEL
MADGE GEISEL
SIMON BRIGHT
AGGIE WHEELER
INSPECTOR GORING
DARIA CHASE

SETTING

The living room of the mansion of William Gillette on the Connecticut River near East Haddam, Connecticut.

TIME

December 1936

AUTHOR'S NOTE

William Gillette was a star of the American stage during the early part of the 20th century. He wrote the play *Sherlock Holmes* in collaboration with Sir Arthur Conan Doyle and he starred in it with enormous success in both New York and London for a total of 1,300 performances spread over thirty years. He became associated with Holmes in the public's imagination; and with his royalties from this and other plays, he built a replica of a medieval castle on the Connecticut River filled with gadgets representing the latest technology. It was here that he entertained the casts of his latest New York hits, and he remained beloved to his fans until his death in his eighties. Gillette Castle is open to the public to this day.

"For murder, though it have no tongue, will speak
With most miraculous organ."

Hamlet, Act 2, Scene 2
William Shakespeare

"Chestnuts roasting on an open fire…"

The Christmas Song
Mel Tormé

ACT ONE

Scene One

(Darkness. Suddenly we hear a furious passage from the fourth movement of Beethoven's String Quartet Opus 95. The volume is high and the passage is nerve-wracking.)

(The time is December 1895. Police whistles rent the air as voices shout "Stop that man!" "Stop him!" "He's a killer!" *A woman screams and the lights come up.)*

(We're in the sitting room of a middle-class house in London at the very moment that a strange man is bolting through the open front door. The chairs and sofa in the room have dust-covers over them, and curtains are drawn over the windows. There is a Christmas tree in one corner, but it has no lights or ornaments on it. A moment later, a second man runs on in pursuit. His name is **SHERLOCK HOLMES**.*)*

HOLMES. *Stop! Moriarty, it's over!*

MORIARTY. *Never!* You'll never catch me, Holmes. I've eluded you this long, and I can assure you that I'm not about to get caught now.

*(***HOLMES*** reaches for his gun – but it's not there! He pats his clothes to find it, but it's gone.* **MORIARTY** *smiles:)*

This afternoon at Doctor Watson's office I took the liberty of relieving you of your gun.

*(***MORIARTY*** pulls out the gun, points it at* **HOLMES** *and pulls the trigger.)*

("Click." It's empty. **MORIARTY** *is shocked.)*

HOLMES. This morning at the gas works I took the liberty of removing the bullets.

15

MORIARTY. Damn you, Holmes!

(**MORIARTY** *throws down the gun and rushes to the back door of the room. He tries to escape, but the door is locked.*)

HOLMES. There is no means of escape this time.

MORIARTY. Of course there is! There's always an escape! In my time I have robbed the Khedive of Egypt. I have emptied the Bank of England. Do you think that I'll surrender to a two-bit consulting detective?!

HOLMES. (*picking up the same gun and pointing it at* **MORIARTY**) I'm afraid you'll have to.

MORIARTY. (*with scorn*) Oh, please. The gun is empty.

(*BANG!* **HOLMES** *has shot the gun within inches of* **MORIARTY**'*s head.*)

HOLMES. I emptied only the first chamber. How else to catch a master criminal?

(**MORIARTY** *looks around wildly for a means of escape – and he sees the open window across the room. He makes a run for it...as* **ALICE** *and* **MARIAN** *rush into the room.*)

ALICE. Mr. Holmes!

MARIAN. Professor!

HOLMES. Don't! Don't do it, it's three stories – !

(*Too late.* **MORIARTY** *has launched himself out the window.*)

MORIARTY. *Ahhhhhh!*

(*He falls with a horrible thud onto the street below. At this moment,* **COUNT ZERLINSKY** *enters. He is dressed in full Hungarian Royal regalia and speaks with a heavy Eastern European accent.*)

ALICE. Oh, Mr. Holmes, thank God you're safe!

COUNT ZERLINSKY. Vell done, vell done, Mr. Holmes!
(*to* **ALICE**) How do you do. Count Zerlinsky.
(*to* **HOLMES** *again*) Come, ve get the letters from the dead body! Ha!

(At the mention of letters, **ALICE** *goes pale.)*

HOLMES. *(quietly)* The letters are not *on* the body. I secured them this morning.

ZERLINSKY. Oh, excellent! Please hand zem over.

HOLMES. I'm afraid I can't do that.

ZERLINSKY. But vhy not?

HOLMES. *(glancing at* **ALICE***)* Because they compromise a young lady who deserves better. A young lady who made one small mistake but will not, I promise you, pay for it for the rest of her life.

ZERLINSKY. But Mister Holmes! The Prince vill be furious.

*(***HOLMES** *shrugs.)*

He vill ruin your reputation! He vill have my head! He vill –

HOLMES. *Get out! Now! I don't want to see you ever again!*

ZERLINSKY. *...Zis iss not over!!*

*(***COUNT ZERLINSKY** *leaves in a huff.)*

MARIAN. Count Zerlinsky! Wait!

(She runs out after him, leaving **ALICE** *and* **HOLMES** *alone in the room.)*

ALICE. Then you did promise to give him the letters.

HOLMES. Yes. And now that you see me in my true light, we have nothing left to say but goodbye. My supposed friendship for you was a pretense, a sham...

ALICE. I don't believe you.

HOLMES. Why not?

ALICE. From the way you speak, from the way you look! You're not the only one who can tell things from small details. Kiss me. Kiss me and then tell me you don't love me.

(He kisses her.)

HOLMES. I...I don't...

(He takes her in his arms and kisses her passionately. Strong music and the curtain falls. We hear the wild applause of an audience – and realize now that what we've just seen is a play within a play. In reality we're at the Palace Theatre in New York City in early December 1936. The curtain rises and the entire cast of five appear and take their bows. Then the man who has been playing **HOLMES** *steps forward and holds up his hand to quiet the crowd.)*

GILLETTE. Ladies and gentlemen, Merry Christmas.

(Audience: "Merry Christmas!")

My name is William Gillette and I thank you for your kind reception of our play about a man of reason who loses his heart and stands up for the one fixed star in his firmament – the cause of justice.

(applause)

As many of you know, I wrote this play some fifteen years ago with the blessing of Sir Arthur Conan Doyle in order to keep his greatest creation – Mr. Sherlock Holmes – alive and well on the stages of the world. Any success we have attained, I attribute entirely to Sir Arthur, though I'm more than happy to bask in his reflected glory.

(laughter; applause)

This was our final performance in New York City, but I hope that you'll come see us again, on tour, which we begin right after Christmas in just –…wait. Stop. Don't anyone move!

(He points into the audience.)

That man has a gun!

(laughter)

No, no, I mean it. I'm not joking. He could be –

(BANG!!! A shot is fired from the audience and **GILLETTE** *cries out and falls to the ground. The actress playing* **ALICE**, *who is beside him, screams, then kneels over him. Her name is* **AGGIE***:)*

AGGIE. *William! William! Please somebody get a doctor!*
THE OTHERS. *Gillette!*

> *William!*
> *There he is!*
> *Stop him!*
> *Find us a doctor!*
> *Bring down the curtain!!*

> *(As the curtain falls and the stage goes black, we hear more of the furious Beethoven quartet. It sets our nerves a-jangle as we transition directly into:)*

Scene Two

(We're in the living room of the home of **WILLIAM GILLETTE,** *two weeks later. It's early evening on Christmas Eve, 1936.)*

(Note: it's actually the same room we saw in the Sherlock Holmes play during Scene One, but the dust covers have come off the furniture, the curtains are pulled back and we're now in the bright, sunny living room of a mansion on the Connecticut River.)

(The room is glamorous, theatrical and extremely hospitable – a whirl of gleaming surfaces and exotic prints, "modern" light fixtures and Art Deco mirrors. Note: it does not *look like the real Gillette Castle interior which is stone and wood. There is nothing dark or medieval about this room. It looks like an Art Deco dream world: full of glass cutouts of glamorous women with hounds; large swaths of color; glamour by the bushel – as though we've stepped into a colorful Erté print. Note: the costumes should match the set. They are all striking and glamorous, each in its own way.)*

(At the moment, the set is decorated for Christmas, so there is a large Christmas tree in one corner, beautifully hung with ornaments and lights, with a number of wrapped presents underneath. There is also tinsel here and there throughout the room, as well as a number of clever and eccentric Santas, snowmen, and Rudolphs.)

(Also, since the house is owned by a hero of melodramas, there are swords and pistols placed dashingly on the walls.)

(There are doors to the hallway stage right and a staircase leading up to a landing [and on up to the bedrooms] stage left. There are French doors at the back leading to a dock. There are at least three other doors in the room: one leading to the dining room, one to the library, and the other one is a closet door. This closet door will play a prominent role during Act One, Scene Two and should not be slighted.)

(During the transition from the London locale to Gillette's living room, we hear a broadcast from a radio on the set. The paragraph in brackets should be cut if the set transition time will allow:)

(Beep-beep-be-beep-beep:)

BROADCASTER. *(unseen)* This is the News of the World for December 1936. Around the country there are lines again, but not for soup anymore, this time it's for jobs aplenty as President Roosevelt fulfills his promise of a New Deal for all Americans.

[Meanwhile, Wallace Simpson, that American gal who changed the course of British history by capturing the heart of a King, was spotted disembarking at the Brooklyn Pier prompting speculation: Is it a New York wedding for these royal lovebirds?]

In entertainment news, Broadway star William Gillette is now recuperating in his Connecticut mansion after that near-fatal shooting on stage at the Palace Theater just two weeks ago. We hear that movie stars galore – including Clark Gable and the glamorous Myrna Loy – have been visiting the great actor in Connecticut, hoping to speed his recovery. For now, we wish him well and look forward to hearing again his famous cry, "Watson! The Game's Afoot!"

*(As the lights come up, **MARTHA** enters from the dining room. She is Gillette's mother, a smartly dressed, somewhat vague and dithering woman in her mid-70s. At the moment, she only has one of her shoes on. She's trying to pull on the other one with little success.)*

(As she opens the door to enter the room, a dog starts barking furiously in the room that she has just left. Perhaps we see a bit of the dog's head darting in and out of the room.)

PORTIA. *Bark, bark, bark, bark, bark!!*

MARTHA. *Down girl!…Stop it!…Portia, I said stop!!*

*(The barking stops. **MARTHA** enters.)*

MARTHA. *(cont.)* Dear little Portia. I love that dog. I wonder how she'd look above the mantlepiece...

(BZZZZZZ! The doorbell buzzes, which sets the dog barking again.)

No! Portia, stop it! Be quiet! Willie! Could you get the door, please, I'm having trouble with my corsage!

*(**GILLETTE** enters from his study. Now that we get to see him properly, we realize that he's a strikingly handsome man, smartly dressed, good-humored, full of irony and life. A sort of modern-day Ulysses. At the moment, he wears an elegant robe, and his arm is in a sling. He carries a beautifully wrapped Christmas present, which he places under the tree.)*

GILLETTE. Sorry, Mother, I'm still in my robe. I simply can't do things as quickly with this damn sling on my arm!

MARTHA. Well then you shouldn't have invited your friends for the weekend. And on Christmas Eve!

GILLETTE. But that makes it festive. Besides, none of them has any other family to speak of.

MARTHA. Oh, *balderdash.* I find this very odd. You were shot just *two weeks ago* and you need to *recover.*

GILLETTE. I am recovered. I'm simply lame at the moment. Like Richard the Third, *"I am not shaped for sportive tricks nor made to court an amorous looking glass."*

MARTHA. Willie, please don't start on one of your –

GILLETTE. *"I am rudely stamped and want love's majesty to strut before a wanton, ambling nymph."*

MARTHA. Willie, this is not the time with people waiting at the –

GILLETTE. *"And that so lamely and unfashionable that dogs bark at me as I halt by them!"*

(BZZZZZ!)

MARTHA. *Willie, will you stop it and get the door!*

GILLETTE. I can't go to the door in my bathrobe, Mother. I'm not eccentric.

(He disappears jauntily up the stairs.)

MARTHA. *(calling up the stairs)* You're a big help!

(BZZZZZ! BZZZZZ!)

I'm coming! It's like living in a madhouse while the gate-keeper is on holiday.

(BZZZZZ! BZZZZZ!)

(She goes to the desk, where she pushes an electric button and speaks into a microphone.)

Hello, who is it?

(We hear **SIMON** *and* **AGGIE** *through the speaker until they enter on the next page.)*

SIMON. It's Simon!

AGGIE. And Aggie!

SIMON. And oh my gosh, is there a speaker in the door or something?

MARTHA. Yes, dear. It's called a speaker-phone and it's one of Willie's hair-brained ideas.

AGGIE. Mrs. Gillette?

MARTHA. Hello, Aggie. How nice to meet you, dear.

SIMON. This is *amazing.* It's like Flash Gordon or something.

AGGIE. Where are *you,* then?

MARTHA. I'm in the drawing room but I'm still getting dressed.

SIMON. You're getting dressed in the drawing room?! Does it have a window so I can watch?

MARTHA. Oh stop it, you terrible boy.

AGGIE. The door seems to be unlocked. Shall we come straight in?

MARTHA. Yes, please. And bring the delinquent with you.

*(***MARTHA*** gets her shoe on and checks her makeup, at which point* **SIMON** *and* **AGGIE** *enter.* **AGGIE,** *who played Alice in the play in Scene One, is a real product of her age: 25, beautiful, bright-eyed and full of spunk.*

She's dressed to perfection in a fur-trimmed coat and muff for the holidays. **SIMON,** *who played Zerlinsky, is sweet and enthusiastic, also 25. They're both innately affectionate and good-natured and make a wonderful couple.)*

AGGIE. *(seeing the room for the first time)* Holy smoke!

SIMON. This is where God would live if he could afford it…

AGGIE. Mrs. Gillette?

MARTHA. Aggie Wheeler, after all this time. I can't believe we haven't met before.

AGGIE. Neither can I.

MARTHA. I've heard all about you from Willie, of course. He simply raves about you.

AGGIE. He's wonderful.

SIMON. Oh doggone it, you've finished dressing!

MARTHA. You wicked creature, get over here.

(They embrace affectionately.)

SIMON. Marry me now. Before the baby arrives.

MARTHA. Oh, you…I've known this young man since he was an extra in *Pride and Prejudice.* I played Mrs. Bennett.

AGGIE. *(taking* **SIMON***'s hand)* I wish I'd seen it.

MARTHA. I pretended I was a little dotty and not all there, you know.

SIMON. It was quite a stretch.

MARTHA. Oh, be quiet.

SIMON. Did you make me a Christmas present? I *love* your presents.

(to **AGGIE***)* Last year she made me her famous peach preserves. I was doubled over with joy for three days.

AGGIE. *(handing* **MARTHA** *a beautifully-wrapped present)* This is for you. Merry Christmas.

MARTHA. Oh, thank you. It looks *beautiful.*

(She puts it under the tree.)

SIMON. This house is amazing! It must have cost the earth.

MARTHA. Oh you know Willie. It's never by halves.

SIMON. When did you move in?

MARTHA. About three months ago now.

AGGIE. And how is he feeling?

MARTHA. Well, he scared me to death getting shot like that, and now he insists he's going to catch the culprit all by himself. I say to him, *"Willie, you're not a policeman!"* But he locks himself up for hours in his laboratory.

SIMON. You have a laboratory?

MARTHA. My dear this house has *everything*. Watch this.

(She pulls a lever and a floor-to-ceiling portion of the bookcase swivels around to create a bar complete with two bar stools and a bar-table. In other words, it's a sort of hidden room within the room that is only revealed when the lever is pulled.)

SIMON. Good Lord.

MARTHA. That's one of his favorites – along with the miniature railroad, the electric snow shovel and the exploding monkey.

(The door bell buzzes.)

That'll be Madge and Felix. I'll be right back.

*(She exits, leaving **AGGIE** and **SIMON** alone in the room. **AGGIE** takes a deep breath.)*

SIMON. Are you holding up all right?

AGGIE. I think so.

SIMON. He'll be fine with it, just trust me.

AGGIE. Right.

SIMON. Good egg.

AGGIE. …You're sure?

SIMON. Absolutely. I want to see their faces when we give them the news. They'll say, "What?! What?!"

*(He makes a face and they laugh happily. At which point, **MADGE** and **FELIX** enter. They played Marian and Moriarty in the play in Scene One. They're in their*

early 40s and married. **FELIX** *is histrionic and arch in a Lionel Barrymore/Sir Toby Belch sort of way.* **MADGE** *is flamboyant and wry in a Rosalind Russell smart-mouthed-gal-about-town sort of way.)*

FELIX. Greetings and salutations!

MADGE. *"What country, friend is this?"*

FELIX. *"It is Illyria, lady."*

MADGE. *"My brother, he is in Elysium. Perchance he is not drowned! What think you, Sailor?"*

FELIX. *"It is perchance that you yourself were saved."* Ha!

(They all embrace and laugh.)

Merry Christmas! Here's to the revels. They shall be non-stop and very drunken. Do you realize that we've been on vacation for a mere two weeks and already I've missed you terribly.

SIMON. Thank you, Felix.

FELIX. Not you, you idiot. Aggie. I've been in love with her since I was uh oh, there's my wife.

MADGE. Keep talking, darling. It will sound so wonderful when it's repeated in court.

AGGIE. How was your time off?

MADGE. Luxurious. We went to a spa. Felix hated it.

FELIX. There was nothing to eat. Or drink! And we had to do some bizarre Buddhist exercise.

MADGE. It's called Yoga.

FELIX. I thought that was the white pudding stuff.

MADGE. That was yoghurt.

FELIX. It was like spoiled milk with the texture of bone marrow. It'll never catch on.

AGGIE. I can't get over this place, can you?

MADGE. He said it was something, but I had no idea.

AGGIE. Why would he build a castle on the Connecticut River?

FELIX. Why does Gillette do anything? The man is insane.

SIMON. I thought he was your best friend.

FELIX. And I repeat, the man is insane.

MADGE. He builds an awfully nice house, though. It would be excellent for a murder.

SIMON. Why a murder?

MADGE. It's isolated, there are loads of rooms for hiding the body, and it's on a river so you can drown people. What more do you want, an ax?

FELIX. *(nodding to the wall)* He has one.

SIMON. Two.

AGGIE. Three.

FELIX. As well as two broadswords, a garrote and a brace of pistols. If Connecticut is ever attacked by Rhode Island, this house will be the first line of defense.

*(They laugh. At which moment, **GILLETTE** enters down the stairs, dressed for the evening.)*

GILLETTE. *And the snow fell gently upon the little stable. And there, in front of it, was a manger made of wood, and in the manger was a boy-child –*

FELIX. *And his name was Sherlock Holmes.*

AGGIE. William!

MADGE. Willie-boy!

GILLETTE. Madge, dear! And Aggie!

AGGIE. How is your arm? Are you in pain?

GILLETTE. Oh it's much better, thank you for asking. Simon, how are you?

SIMON. It's good to see you, sir.

GILLETTE. I see you've all arrived safely, despite wind and weather.

SIMON. It's getting pretty dicey out there.

GILLETTE. "Blow winds," eh? "and crack your cheeks."

FELIX. *"Spout / Till you have drenched our steeples, drowned the cocks!"*

GILLETTE. *"But even then the morning cock crew loud
And at the sound it shrunk in haste away."*

FELIX. *"The knave turns fool that runs away."*

GILLETTE. *"Where's my fool? Ho! I think the world's asleep!"*

FELIX. *"To sleep, perchance to dream."*

GILLETTE. *"To sleep, no more."*

MADGE. Fault! You repeated "sleep." Game, set and match to Felix.

FELIX. My God I love you.

MADGE. Of course you do.

FELIX. Ha!

GILLETTE. Felix, you scoundrel! Were you making fun of me down here?

FELIX. Moi?

GILLETTE. I do have the proof.

> (**GILLETTE** *looks heavenward and we hear voices coming through a speaker:*)
>
> (**AGGIE:** *Why would he build a castle on the Connecticut River?*)
>
> (**FELIX***: Why does* **GILLETTE** *do anything? The man is insane.*)
>
> (**SIMON***: I thought he was your best friend.*)
>
> (**FELIX***: And I repeat, the man is insane.*)

FELIX. What in God's name was that?

GILLETTE. My latest goody. Microphones here and here, and I can turn them on and off at all the light switches.

SIMON. How do you play it back?

> (**GILLETTE** *takes a remote control device from his pocket and holds it up. It's large and distinctive-looking.*)

GILLETTE. It's called a "remote control." First presented in 1903 to the Paris Academy of Science and under development ever since. It sends signals through the air without wires. The military is starting to use them.

SIMON. You're amazing!

> (**MARTHA** *enters with a tray of champagne glasses.*)

MARTHA. Hello, my darlings. I've brought some bubbly so we can *really* celebrate.

MADGE. Now you're talking!

FELIX. Here, let me help. That looks awfully heavy.

(She gives him a kiss as he takes the tray.)

MARTHA. You darling boy. He always looks after me. Unlike some children I know who will remain unnamed.

GILLETTE. "*An ill-favored thing, sir, but mine own.*"

MARTHA. Oh stop blathering, Willie. He can be so irritating. Especially since he got shot – he's so proud of it. By the way, where's Barnes? I can't find him anywhere.

AGGIE. Who's Barnes?

MARTHA. He's our butler. Can you imagine, we have a butler!

GILLETTE. I gave him the night off.

MARTHA. What?!

GILLETTE. He looked tired, and we're all family, really.

MARTHA. Oh, Willie, how could you?! With your bad arm you can't even help me!

GILLETTE. Oh of course I can. Look: I've been meaning to do this for two days now.

(He takes off his sling. Handing it to **FELIX***:)*

Here. Frame it.

FELIX. We'll call it *A Farewell to Arms*.

SIMON. I suppose there's been no progress finding the man who shot you.

GILLETTE. Well, the police are stuck, but I believe I've found something.

OTHERS. What? / But what? / What is it?

GILLETTE. *(pulling out an envelope)* Do you remember the note that was left at the stage door on the day of the shooting?

SIMON. The stage door?

AGGIE. *I* do. Old Noggsy told me the envelope was addressed to you, but the note was blank.

GILLETTE. Exactly. And the police lost interest in it.

(He pulls a Bunsen burner from under his desk and places it on the coffee table. During the following, he lights it and everyone gathers around.)

But I've been subjecting it to some tests upstairs in my laboratory, and in the end it was a matter of trial and error. Take a look.

(He holds the note over the flame, etc.)

It took a few tries, but I mixed a little sodium carbonate into the alcohol, so it isn't just the heat that's doing it, it's also the chemical...

SIMON. Oh my gosh.

AGGIE. Look!

(Writing has appeared on the paper.)

FELIX. *(taking the note)* "Dear Mr. Holmes,
Bang, you're dead."

SIMON. Then they *were* trying to kill you.

AGGIE. Wait! There's more. Look.
(reading) "H-V-I-I-I-1-3-5." It's like a cipher.

SIMON. Maybe it's a German code. I mean with Hitler and all...

GILLETTE. Possibly. On the other hand – Aggie, could you please hand me that Shakespeare on the bookstand? You see, most people don't realize that when Sherlock Holmes says "The game is afoot" in the "Adventure of the Abbey Grange," he is in fact quoting Shakespeare.

AGGIE. Which play?

SIMON. H-V-I-I-I...*Henry the Eighth!*

FELIX. That's a wonderful guess, Simon, but it's wrong.

MADGE. Henry the Fifth.

FELIX. Of course.

MADGE. *"Once more unto the breach, dear friends, once more,
Or close the wall up with our English dead!"*

FELIX. *"I see you stand like greyhounds in the slips,
Straining upon the start."*

FELIX & MADGE. *"THE GAME'S AFOOT!"*

AGGIE. So "H-V" is Henry the Fifth.

SIMON. And "I-I-I-1-3-5" is

GILLETTE. Act 3, scene 1, line 35.

> *(showing them a page in the book:)*

> At the marking.

AGGIE. *"The game's afoot."* Wow.

SIMON. It was left for you at the stage door? That's rather creepy.

FELIX. But what does it mean?

MADGE. It means whoever tried to kill you is seriously crazy.

FELIX. *(looking at* **GILLETTE***)* There's something more, isn't there? Let me see that.

> *(He takes the letter and holds it up to the light, peering at it)*

> There's a watermark.

SIMON. What's a watermark?

GILLETTE. An impression pressed into the paper when it's manufactured.

MADGE. A sort of advertisement. Hotels do it, and businesses.

FELIX. Oh, Christ.

SIMON. What?

MADGE. Where is it from?

FELIX. The Palace Theater.

MADGE. Oh, no.

AGGIE. I'm not following this.

MADGE. It means whoever wrote this had access to the theater's stationery. It means they worked at our theater.

> *(They look at each other with uneasiness.)*

SIMON. ...It could have been someone from the stage crew...

AGGIE. Or a producer.

FELIX. Or an actor.

(Silence. The mood is tense. You could cut it with a knife.)

MARTHA. Well, you've certainly made it a jolly Christmas, Willie.

GILLETTE. Oh, stop it. We shouldn't jump to conclusions. Someone could have swiped the paper, in which case no one here is involved at all.

(General relief. The following lines overlap: "That's true." "Of course it is." "It's like a beehive backstage.")

Ladies and Gentlemen, to the Swiper!

(They laugh.)

Cheers!

ALL. Cheers! / Merry Christmas! / To us!

(They drink.)

SIMON. Uh, while we have the drinks out and we're feeling jolly and all, I'd uh like to make an announcement, if I may. Well...

AGGIE. Go on.

SIMON. Well, Aggie and I are married.

MADGE. What?

FELIX. What?

MARTHA. You mean engaged.

AGGIE. No, married. Four weeks ago.

*(They all erupt happily – except **GILLETTE**.)*

MADGE/FELIX/MARTHA. Oh, Simon! Aggie! / You're kidding! / That's wonderful!

MARTHA. He tells me nothing. My son tells me nothing at all!

SIMON. We were going to tell all of you after the run, but then the shooting happened –

MARTHA. Oh it's marvelous.

*(to **GILLETTE**)* Isn't it wonderful, dear?

GILLETTE. Hm? Yes. Of course it is. Absolutely.

MARTHA. *(to* **AGGIE***:)* And you're so *brave* to get married again after what happened the *last time.*

(Dead silence.)

GILLETTE. Mother…

MARTHA. Well she is. I mean her husband died on their honeymoon, didn't he? That's what I heard.

GILLETTE. Mother, for heaven's sake –

AGGIE. Yes, he did die, Mrs. Gillette, and I don't mind talking about it. In fact talking about it makes it more bearable.

MARTHA. *(to* **GILLETTE***)* There. Are you satisfied?

(to **AGGIE***)* Now tell us what happened. I want to know *everything.*

AGGIE. There isn't really much to tell. Hugo and I – that was my husband – we were married just over a year ago, and we went to Killington in Vermont to ski for our honeymoon.

MARTHA. Did you really? I hear that's *very* expensive.

MADGE. Her husband was quite well off.

MARTHA. That's what I heard. They say he was *loaded.* One of the richest men in the entire –

GILLETTE. That's it. I give up.

MARTHA. Oh Willie, stop it. I hate it when people beat around the bush. It's like you and Penelope. You were married, she died, you miss her and there's an end to it. And it makes you feel better when we talk about it, doesn't it?

GILLETTE. *(with a rueful smile at his mother's wisdom)* …Yes it does.

MARTHA. *Thank* you.

(to **AGGIE***)* Go on, my dear. Spill the beans.

AGGIE. Well…my husband was an excellent skier, but he decided to try the Black Diamond slope, which is the most dangerous one at the resort. He got all dressed in his jacket and goggles and the attendant tightened his gloves and boots and Hugo set off down the hill, as happy as I've ever seen him...and then...

MARTHA. Yes?

AGGIE. The strap on his boot just...broke while he was coming down the hill, and...the ski sort of came apart or something, and he lost control on the iciest part of the slope and he...he hit a tree and died instantly.

MARTHA. Oh, no.

AGGIE. I must have been in shock at first because I tried to just...talk to people and pretend that things were manageable...but by the end of the first night I was shaking so hard I couldn't stop.

MARTHA. And you were all alone.

SIMON. Well, not for long. She had the good sense to wire me that night. We've been best friends for ages, and I was in a show in New York at the time –

AGGIE. And he dropped everything and arrived the next day. He was a great comfort.

MARTHA. And the rest is history. How romantic.

FELIX. In a lugubrious sort of way.

MADGE. Don't you start. Martha's right. You have to face up to life. No matter what the world throws at you, no matter how difficult it can get sometimes, you just have to say to hell with the bastards and go on living.

FELIX. That's my girl. Let's cheer things up with a little music, shall we?

(He heads for the radio.)

SIMON. Here, here!

MADGE. To the happy couple!

ALL. The happy couple!

*(**FELIX** turns on the radio and tries to find a good tune. But he only finds opera and news broadcasts...and meanwhile, **SIMON** has found a ukulele lying about. He starts to play: and he and **AGGIE** sing a popular song*

*of the era — something upbeat and fun, like "DeLovely"
or "Anything Goes" by Cole Porter or "I Got Rhythm" by
George Gershwin.* They all start dancing and enjoying
themselves. Being actors, their dancing is joyful and a
bit loony. Then, without warning, we hear the ominous
sound of a ship's horn from the direction of the river.)*

GILLETTE. Wait. Wait! Hold on for a moment.

(He turns the volume of the radio down.)

I believe that our final guest has arrived and she's pulling into the dock this minute.

FELIX. There's someone else?

MARTHA. Who is it?

GILLETTE. Guess.

MARTHA. Oh, Willie…

AGGIE. Is she in the show?

GILLETTE. No, not in the show, but in show *business.*

SIMON. Do we know her?

GILLETTE. Well you certainly know *of* her.

FELIX. I smell trouble.

MARTHA. Willie, would you stop being coy! My God, he
could drive Saint Joan to drink. Just tell us who it is!

GILLETTE. …It's Daria Chase.

(Silence. **FELIX** *turns the music off.)*

SIMON. What?

AGGIE. Oh no.

MARTHA. Oh, Willie, how could you.

SIMON. She's awful.

FELIX. She's worse than that.

MARTHA. I met her at a party once and she *completely*
snubbed me.

FELIX. She gave me the worst review I ever had in my life. It
was a costume drama with Joan Crawford, no less. She
said, "The radiant Miss Crawford came on to the click-
ing of high heels followed by a lump of roast beef."

---

*Please see Music Use Note on Page 3.

MADGE. She said I played Hamlet's mother looking like a worried hamster.

SIMON. I was in a play last year and appeared in a bathing suit. She wrote: "Simon Bright's audacity in the role was largely in excess of his equipment."

GILLETTE. Well, she's clever at least.

FELIX. She's a spiteful, gossip-mongering harridan bitch and you owe us all an explanation.

ALL. Here, here. / I agree. *(etc.)*

GILLETTE. All right, fine. She's writing a profile of me for *Vanity Fair* and she asked to come to one of our weekends. Now like it or not, Daria Chase is the most influential columnist in the country. Her profile of me will give us more free publicity than if I'd shot Lincoln. So I suggest that as a courtesy to me you are at least civil to Miss Chase and that you get off your fannies and go greet her at the dock. Thank you.

(Everyone heads for the door to the garden.)

SIMON. Exit ungrateful guests shuffling feet.

*(**SIMON, MARTHA, FELIX** and **MADGE** exit – but before leaving, **FELIX** adds a last word to **GILLETTE**:)*

FELIX. You're up to something, aren't you?

*(**FELIX** rolls his eyes and leaves. **GILLETTE** turns back to the room – and sees that **AGGIE** has lingered to talk to **GILLETTE** privately.)*

GILLETTE. You didn't tell me.

AGGIE. I couldn't. I didn't have the courage.

GILLETTE. Courage?

AGGIE. I didn't want you to think less of me.

GILLETTE. But Simon is a fine fellow.

AGGIE. He's more than that!

GILLETTE. What I mean is –

AGGIE. I know what you mean. He's ordinary. He's "nice." He's easy to please. Well he *is* those things. And he's in love with me.

GILLETTE. Are you in love with him?

AGGIE. *(hurt)* Of course I am. I wouldn't have married him otherwise. *(increasingly upset)* And he's very, very kind. When I needed him, he was there in an instant.

GILLETTE. Of course he was.

AGGIE. But I was in love with you. You just…you didn't ask me. I gave you every chance. I offered you everything!

GILLETTE. I know you did. And I was too foolish to take you up on it. I had some misguided notion that I was being loyal to my wife's memory.

AGGIE. It's been ten years since your wife died.

GILLETTE. Yes, I know.

AGGIE. *(in his arms)* Oh, William…

GILLETTE. Aggie, listen. You're going to be fine. The best man won. I'm sure of it. And for heaven's sake, just look at me. I'm old enough to be your slightly older brother.

(She laughs nervously.)

AGGIE. Thanks. Thanks a million.…It's just that I…I mean, I thought that you…felt something…

(almost breaking down)

You treat everything as a joke! Even that horrible attempt on your life!

GILLETTE. Not as a joke, my dear, but as a game, which is a different thing entirely. Look, we have chosen this mad life of ours, and we'd be insane not to accept it for what it is. Do I go to an office? No. Do I wear a tie to work? No. We're actors. We wear silly costumes. We put on noses made of putty, for God's sake. We don't want to be grownups. We're all Peter Pans and a good thing it is too. I don't want to leave all the fun behind because I've reached some magical age of regret. That's what they want us to do, you know, all those gray faceless accountants, and I won't do it. I won't. I don't treat life as a joke – I treat it as the most glorious game ever invented. Love and heartbreak? Game. Life and death?

GILLETTE. *(cont.)* The greatest game, the biggest adventure. Shakespeare got it right on the nose. Henry the Fifth charging into battle against overwhelming odds and what does he cry? *"It's all a game and if I die, I die!"* So let them praise me, hate me or shoot at me – but at the end of the battle, I will have *lived,* even for a moment. And if you think you need Simon in order to live like that, then take him, by all means! Cling to him! Don't hesitate for a second!…I will, however, miss you unutterably.

(Beat. **AGGIE** *is speechless. Her heart starts racing and she realizes how much she loves him. She leans in to kiss him – when sounds from the terrace interrupt the moment.)*

FELIX. *(off)* Gillette! Guess who's here?! It's our old friend Daria Chase!

*(***DARIA CHASE*** *enters, followed by the others.* **DARIA** *is gorgeous, glamorous, and dressed to the nines with holiday chic. She's one of those people you can't take your eyes off of; and despite all of her show-biz cattiness, you can't help liking her – or at least admiring her. She has a sense of humor and has invented herself from the ground up, which is no mean feat.)*

DARIA. *(She poses.)* Merry Christmas! Oh William! My dear, sweet, vulnerable man! How is your *arm?* Your *heart?* Your *soul? Ah!* After that ghastly shooting I thought I'd never see you again! That or I'd find you limping like a broken lion to the final watering hole.

GILLETTE. And here I am as right as rain and twice as healthy. Daria, you look magnificent.

DARIA. Oh, please. I simply grabbed whatever was hanging in my sad, little closet as I bounded out of New York City for the countryside on *Christmas Eve* and oh my God just smell the air out here! I haven't smelled air like this since I was a little girl growing up in Kansas or wherever it was with all those divine little cows and things. How lucky you are to have all this…nature to comfort you.

FELIX. Just like that famous painting on the grass, but with our clothes on.

DARIA. Oh, Felix, my dear, how *are* you?

FELIX. Not as well as you, obviously.

DARIA. Oh stop it. My beauty is superficial and yours is on the inside. And Madge. My God we go back a ways, don't we? I remember when I first came to New York as a youngster – how I looked up to you with all your years of experience.

MADGE. And yet my friends and I called you "Mother."

DARIA. Now stop it, that's impossible. You didn't have any friends.

MADGE. I had Felix.

DARIA. And didn't everyone.

GILLETTE. Daria, let me introduce the rest of the clan. This is my mother, Martha Gillette.

MARTHA. We've met before. Very briefly, at a party. But I do read your column. In fact, I keep it right next to my bed in case I can't get to sleep at night.

GILLETTE. Mother!

DARIA. What a witty thing to say. And so unexpected.

SIMON. Hello, Daria. It's nice to see you.

DARIA. Simon, my dear, you're looking very well.

SIMON. As do you!

GILLETTE. I didn't know that you two –

DARIA. Of course we do. We met at Killington, at the big weekend. I was there for the skiing and those divine parties.

(*to* **AGGIE***)* Then after I left, your husband had that ghastly accident, didn't he. I was so upset. If I had stayed I would have had one of the biggest scoops of the whole year! And poor you. It must have been quite upsetting.

MADGE. I'll bet you don't know they're married now.

AGGIE. For four weeks.

SIMON. Four weeks, two days, and six hours. I'm especially proud of the six hours. It shows I can really stick with it.

DARIA. The truth is, I do know about it, and I plan to put it in my column on Monday morning. I mean, just look at the two of you. You're headline news! One minute you're character actors, the next minute you've inherited half of the Pacific Northwest.

SIMON. What do you mean?

DARIA. What do I – ? Darling, you've just married the Merry Widow of Manhattan for God's sake.

SIMON. Sorry, but you've got it wrong. Hugo didn't leave her anything.

DARIA. *Excuse me*, but I *am* a reporter. When I found the records on your marriage, I happened to see Hugo's will and testament.

(to **AGGIE***:)* He left you everything, didn't he? All his millions.

AGGIE. ....Yes, he did.

(The room erupts.)

FELIX, MARTHA & MADGE. Oh my God!/That's amazing!/ Oh, Aggie!/Simon!

GILLETTE. Why didn't you tell us?

AGGIE. I-I don't know. I-I didn't want it to affect my relationship with anyone. They'd treat me differently, you know they would.

SIMON. Does this mean I'm rich?

*(***AGGIE*** nods.)*

Very rich?

(Nod.)

Hahaaaaaaaaaaaaaaaa! I'm rich, I'm rich, I'm rich! How do you do? I'm rich. You may touch me...

(He rushes to **AGGIE***, but stops abruptly:)*

You just made my day.

(He embraces her and they all laugh.)

DARIA. I must say, this cast of yours gives me endless things to write about. It's like I *invented* you just for the purpose.

MADGE. We'd rather you wrote about the play and not us.

DARIA. Oh, nonsense. Of course you wouldn't. Everyone wants publicity. It's magic, and it's changing the world. Look at me, I'm a sorceress. A wave of the pen and I can make you a star. Poof. Publicity equals fame equals money. It's like a drug, but it never stops. And I must say, you've all been hogging the limelight beautifully, haven't you. First the shooting, which in itself must have doubled my readership, then the inheritance and now the *murder* –

FELIX. Murder?

AGGIE. What murder?

SIMON. You mean the shooting.

DARIA. No, I mean the murder this morning.

(Dead silence.)

Don't tell me you don't…

*(to **GILLETTE**)* Do *you* know about it?

GILLETTE. I'm afraid I do. I was going to tell everyone *after* dinner.

DARIA. Oops.

AGGIE. Who was murdered?

GILLETTE. Noggs.

(Shocked silence.)

SIMON. Stage doorman Noggs?

GILLETTE. I'm afraid so.

AGGIE. Oh no.

GILLETTE. The police asked me to identify the body this morning. It happened late last night, apparently.

DARIA. I was there.

GILLETTE. Excuse me?

DARIA. At your theater. Last night. Not *at* the murder, of course.

MADGE. But there's no show on at the moment.

DARIA. I was doing background work on my article.

FELIX. Did you see Noggs there?

DARIA. Yes, I did. When I went *in,* but he was murdered apparently when I was inside.

SIMON. But who would murder him? I mean – poor Noggsy.

MARTHA. Perhaps he saw something related to the shooting. Or overheard someone talking about it.

AGGIE. Could it have been an accident?

SIMON. Or natural causes, like a heart attack.

GILLETTE. That would be very comforting indeed, except his throat was cut from ear to ear with a razor blade.

(BOOM!! A thunderclap. They all jump. Through the windows we can see the snow falling.)

MADGE. There's a storm brewing.

FELIX. And I have a feeling it's going to get quite nasty before it's over.

MARTHA. Oh nonsense, it's Christmas Eve, now let's have dinner. Right this way. Let's go everybody!

*(***MARTHA*** opens the door to the dining room, and Portia starts barking again.)*

PORTIA. *Bark, bark, bark, bark, bark!!*

MARTHA. *Oh, Portia, be quiet!*

(Everyone starts filing into the dining room chatting.)

DARIA. *(winding* **FELIX***'s arm around hers)* Felix, my darling, will you take me in? I'm like the maiden aunt of the family, all sad and lonely.

FELIX. *(glancing at* **MADGE***)* ...Of course.

*(***DARIA*** and **FELIX** go in.)*

SIMON. *(taking* **AGGIE***'s arm, imitating Daria)* Aggie, my darling, will you take me in? I'm like the bachelor uncle of the family, all full of myself and annoying...

AGGIE. Shh! Stop it! She'll hear you!

(**SIMON** *and* **AGGIE** *go in.* **GILLETTE** *goes to the radio.*)

GILLETTE. *(aloud, so that everyone hears him)* Let's leave the doors open so we can hear the music, shall we?

(*Everyone has gone by this time except* **MADGE**, *who has lingered. She waits to make sure that she and* **GILLETTE** *are alone, then says quietly:*)

MADGE. Are we still going through with it?

GILLETTE. Absolutely.

(**GILLETTE** *turns on the radio and then accompanies* **MADGE** *into the dining room, leaving the living room empty.*)

(*The Beethoven string quartet resumes ferociously, drowning out the radio. As the stage goes black, we hear another huge clap of thunder and see a flash of lightning.*)

End of Scene

Scene Three

(The same room, an hour later.)

(The scene begins with more Beethoven, the same quartet, as disturbing as ever. Then comes a boom of thunder and a flash of lightning, and we see a blizzard of snowflakes lashing at the windows.)

*(As the lights come up, **AGGIE** is alone in the room. She's looking wistfully at some memento of Gillette, perhaps a painting of him, or a piece of Sherlockiana. We hear laughter coming from the dining room.)*

*(After a moment, **FELIX** enters from the dining room.)*

FELIX. I'll be right back.

GILLETTE. *(off)* Hurry it up!

SIMON. *(off)* We want dessert!

*(**FELIX** closes the door behind him and then sees **AGGIE**.)*

FELIX. Aggie, dear. Are you all right?

AGGIE. I was looking around…It's beautiful here, isn't it.

FELIX. Spectacular, but that's William, isn't it. He likes the best, and he usually gets it. But not always.

AGGIE. I had no idea he was this successful.

FELIX. He's taken us all by surprise, actually. He and I started out together, we were roommates in the city – both of us as poor as church mice, auditioning for everything that came along. Then one day, out of the blue, he says, "I think I'll write a play about Sherlock Holmes," and I say, "Don't be ridiculous, that'll *never* work." So he writes the play and stars in it and it runs for twenty years and here we are.

AGGIE. I know he admires you tremendously.

FELIX. Does he?

*(Do we sense some jealousy in **FELIX**'s reply? It's not impossible. **DARIA** appears at the top of the stairs and sweeps down.)*

DARIA. Well, well, well, if it isn't the Heiress of Brooklyn.

AGGIE. Hello.

DARIA. Do you know, I've been thinking about what happened to you. Pretty young actress, no money, meets eligible young man who's very rich. He falls deeply in love with her, marries her and promptly dies on the honeymoon and I think to myself: you must be the luckiest girl in the entire world.

FELIX. Daria, she lost her husband, for heaven's sake.

DARIA. Oh, please. Husbands are a dime a dozen. They come and go like ducks around a country pond. They waddle around looking self-important, they quack as though someone is actually listening to them, and then, mercifully, they die off and disappear.

AGGIE. I think I should go now.

(**AGGIE** *exits into the dining room.*)

FELIX. That was very endearing of you, Daria. Why not just take an ax and chop her feet off.

DARIA. Oh, grow up. The little gold-digger hit the jackpot. What more does she want, a trophy? And she got Simon in the bargain. Now let's stop talking about them. Let's talk about me instead. What is it you like most about me?

FELIX. Your shyness.

DARIA. I like you because you're handsome. And stoic. Doesn't all of Gillette's success make you want to scream? Aren't you seething inside with jealousy?

FELIX. No, he's my best friend.

DARIA. *Really?* You didn't try to shoot him, then.

FELIX. How could I? I was on stage when he was shot.

DARIA. So was everybody who's here this weekend. Except dear, innocent Martha.

FELIX. And you.

DARIA. Why would I want to shoot him? I haven't slept with him yet. Now stop being stoic and kiss me.

FELIX. I'm a married man.

DARIA. *(cuddling up to him)* You mean your lips don't work at all any more?

FELIX. Daria…

DARIA. Ten minutes, upstairs, they'd never miss us.

FELIX. Daria!

DARIA. We never get to spend time together!

FELIX. We could be spending a great deal of time together, in there eating dinner.

DARIA. You're angry about the review, aren't you?

FELIX. You did call me a side of beef.

DARIA. But in a nice way! Oh, Felix, I was just trying to get a laugh. I should tell the truth when I write, shouldn't I? Truth and beauty, as the poet Shelley said: it is all we know on earth and all we need to know.

FELIX. Keats.

DARIA. Hmm?

FELIX. It was the poet Keats.

DARIA. You know, Felix, you're even more attractive when you stand up to me.

(She kisses him hungrily on the lips and really goes at it. Then she breaks it off.)

FELIX. I should get back to the others.

DARIA. Not yet, surely.

FELIX. Daria.

(She whimpers.)

Daria, down!

DARIA. You know, Felix, there are certain things I know about your past that you might not want bandied about among your loved ones. So it might be in your best interests to be nicer to me, don't you *think?*

*(We see a flash of anger cross **FELIX**'s face – as the door of the dining room bursts open and **GILLETTE** enters, leading his guests.)*

SIMON/MADGE/AGGIE/MARTHA. A wonderful dinner! /It really was! / Kudos to the hostess. / Thank you, thank you.

GILLETTE. *(to* **FELIX***)* Ah, Philostrate! Master of the Revels!
Stir up the Athenian youth to merriment,
Awake the pert and nimble spirit of mirth!

FELIX. I shall turn melancholy forth to funerals, now get out the cards so we can play some bridge.

MADGE. I vote for pinochle.

SIMON. Charades!

AGGIE. Dancing!

GILLETTE. Oh come, come! I have something planned that's better than all those put together. I'll give you a hint. It involves shimmering images.

MARTHA. Oh, Willie…

MADGE. Here he goes again.

SIMON. You have a screening room like they do in Hollywood.

GILLETTE. No, but a good guess.

FELIX. A slide show.

AGGIE. A walk in the moonlight!

(We hear a clap of thunder and the howl of wind.)

GILLETTE. Clever, but unlikely under the circumstances.

MARTHA. Oh, what is it, Willie?! You are so aggravating.

GILLETTE. Well…what do you *say* to a…séance?

(beat)

AGGIE. A séance?

GILLETTE. *"When churchyards yawn and hell itself breathes out Contagion to this world!"*

SIMON. Do you mean like holding hands and talking to the dead?

GILLETTE. We don't say dead, we say "passed over."

FELIX. Or we say "lunatic head of acting company forces guests through traumatic evening."

AGGIE. Are you really a believer?

GILLETTE. Yes. That is, I'm getting to be. Conan Doyle got me started and he's quite fanatical about it.

SIMON. But don't we need a "medium" or something?

GILLETTE. We do indeed. And tonight we have the best in the business. Daria?

FELIX. I knew it! I knew you were up to something!

DARIA. I'm warning you all, right now, that I take this very seriously.

SIMON. But when did you…?

DARIA. I've been a medium since I was fifteen. I was staying in Paris with my aunt and uncle who were in grief over the loss of their daughter, my cousin Clemence. The family dabbled in these things, and one night they included me in their ceremony. They were trying to contact Clemence and having no luck when suddenly, without warning, she started speaking through me, through my lips.

SIMON. That must have hurt.

DARIA. It was exhilarating.

AGGIE. But why have a séance tonight? Who are we contacting?

GILLETTE. Guesses?

FELIX. Noggs.

MARTHA. Dear old Noggsy.

SIMON. But why?

FELIX. Because, dear boy, he must have overheard something in one of the dressing rooms – the plot to kill Gillette, presumably. So if he tells us what he saw or heard, or the name of the person who slit his throat, then the mystery is solved. Am I right?

GILLETTE. Exactly.

SIMON. Does that mean we're all suspects?

GILLETTE. Oh not at all. He might say it was the understudy. Or the wardrobe mistress.

FELIX. Or my Aunt Fanny.

GILLETTE. *(clapping his hands)* Let's go, let's go.

DARIA. The table will be our center, our portal. Please bring a chair.

(A bit of hubbub here: **MADGE, MARTHA, FELIX** *and* **AGGIE** *start moving the furniture.)*

ALL. This one, I think. / How's this? / That's fine. / We'll put this one here…

(Meanwhile, **GILLETTE** *has a side conversation with* **SIMON** *that no one else hears:)*

GILLETTE. Incidentally, you had a call this afternoon from a young woman. She said her name was Tamsin.

SIMON. Oh no.

GILLETTE. Is there a problem?

SIMON. No. Well. She was a friend of mine – a girlfriend actually. She knows that I'm married now, but she persists in calling me. It's crazy.

GILLETTE. Is she unbalanced?

SIMON. No…I don't *think* so. I hope not…

GILLETTE. Does Aggie know about it?

SIMON. Yes, and she understands it's not my fault. At least I think she does…

DARIA. I believe we're ready.

GILLETTE. Excellent! Tell us what to do.

DARIA. All right, now I want each of you to stay exactly where you are and take a deep breath. Good. Now look around and feel the presence of the other persons in this room. Look at your friends and where they're standing, how they look…Very good. Now I'm going to lower the lights, and I want each of you to take a seat around the table, anywhere you please.

(She lowers the lights; and we hear a rumble of thunder.)

SIMON. I'm beginning to feel creepy already.

FELIX. You *are* creepy already.

MADGE. Be quiet!

AGGIE. Shhh!

DARIA. Now I'm putting some music on just to calm things down. The mood in the room is very important.

(She turns the radio on at a low volume and we hear a Christmas tune.)

Let the mood relax you. Let it enter your bodies. Slowly. Deeply.

SIMON. I could get used to this...

AGGIE. Does it always work? I mean are you always successful in...reaching someone?

DARIA. Oh not at all. Quite the contrary. All we can do is create the proper atmosphere so that someone from the other side will want to join us.

SIMON. We could serve drinks.

DARIA. ...My contact is a young actress who was murdered by her husband in 1820 in London after a performance of *Othello*. He thought she was committing adultery with her leading man.

FELIX. Life imitates art.

MADGE. Isn't *that* comforting.

(silence)

DARIA. Now put your hands on the table. Fingers touching.

(They do. We hear another rumble of thunder and see the snow blowing against the windows. The room is dark.)

(silence)

(The atmosphere is building.)

SIMON. My name is Count Drah –cu – lahhh...

*(**DARIA** begins to spring up, but **GILLETTE** puts his hand on hers and restrains her.)*

Sorry. I couldn't help it. Sorry.

*(**DARIA** takes a breath and reins herself in. The atmosphere builds again. **DARIA** closes her eyes. The atmosphere is thick with foreboding and uncertainty. Finally:)*

DARIA. Laurentia? *[pronounced "Lor-en-cha."]* ...Are you there?

(Silence. Nothing.)

Laurentia, dear, this is Daria. Could you come and visit us?

(nothing)

Laurentia, I think you'll like this visit because you'll be doing someone a big favor.

(silence)

(Then suddenly, finally, there's a loud KNOCK from under the table. Everyone cries out in surprise.)

ALL. *Oh!*

FELIX. Good God!

MADGE. Shhh!

AGGIE. Simon, stop fooling around!

SIMON. It wasn't me!

DARIA. Is that you, Laurentia?

(KNOCK!)

FELIX. I think we should put a stop to this –

MADGE. Oh don't be a baby.

FELIX. I'm telling you this is a bad idea –

DARIA. *Would you two be quiet!*...Laurentia: thank you for coming. I deeply appreciate it.

(...KNOCK!)

Now Laurentia, listen carefully. Someone named Noggs, the stage doorman at the Palace Theater in New York City was murdered recently and we're hoping that you can bring him here so we can ask him some questions. Are you willing to help us, Laurentia?

(Pause. KNOCK!)

Thank you, my darling. Is there anything you would like *us* to do?

(Knock, knock, knock, knock!!! The table starts wobbling furiously and everyone is surprised and frightened.)

ALL. *Ah! / Hold it down! / I'm trying!! / What is she doing?!*

DARIA. *STOP IT, LAURENTIA!!* Put your hands on the table. Keep the connection.

(The table settles down.)

Now is there anything you'd like to say, dear?... Laurentia?...Are you still there?...Laurentia, please...

*(Slowly, **MADGE** stands up, breathing heavily and with difficulty. Her mouth is agape, her eyes are distant and unfocused and her head is thrown back at a peculiar angle. She seems possessed by a spirit that is not her own. In the darkness, with the shadows on her face and on the walls, the effect is weird and disturbing. She speaks in a guttural sound that is not her own voice:)*

MADGE. *Murder.*

(Everyone turns and gasps.)

Murder!

FELIX. Madge...?

MADGE. *(She raises her hand and points straight at **SIMON**.) Confess or die.*

SIMON. What?

AGGIE. Simon?

SIMON. I didn't do anything!

MADGE. *Confess or die!!*

SIMON. Stop doing that! I have nothing to confess!

*(She swivels and points straight at **AGGIE**.)*

MADGE. *Confess or diiiiie.*

AGGIE. *Stop it!*

SIMON. *Leave her alone!*

AGGIE. *Simon, make her stop!*

FELIX. Madge, stop this nonsense at once. I don't believe it for a single sec –

AGGIE. *She's not pointing at you! She's pointing out the window!*

(They all turn away from **MADGE** *and look out the window.)*

SIMON. *Where?!*

DARIA. *Through there!*

AGGIE. *I think someone's out there!!*

FELIX. *Who is it?!*

MADGE. *AAAAAAAAAAAAAAHHHHHHHHHHHHHHHH HHHHHHH!*

(Everyone turns quickly to look back at **MADGE** *– and she has a large knife sticking out of her chest. There is a look of terrifying shock on her face and for a moment, everything seems frozen in time. There's a loud boom of thunder – and* **MADGE** *convulses forward. A stream of blood shoots out of her mouth and she falls forward onto the table with a thud.)*

(Everyone is screaming by this time.)

ALL. *Madge! Oh my God! Madge, darling! / Call an ambulance! / Is she still alive?! / Help her up! / Somebody do something!*

GILLETTE. *NO, DON'T TOUCH HER!*

(Silence. Everyone stares at him in shock.)

Whoever killed Noggs is next, so for God's sake confess it now....*Confess it, I beg you!!*

(No response.)

No one?

(beat)

MADGE. Well...

*(***MADGE** *stands up and pulls the knife out of her chest.)*

THE OTHERS. *Ahhhhhhhhhh!*

MADGE. That didn't work very well, now did it.

GILLETTE. It was a good try, though.

MADGE. Except now we're going to get yelled at, I can feel it.

FELIX. Madge...?

MADGE. I'm sorry, darling, it was his idea. And we had this knife left over from that production of *The Maid of Turkey*, and the blood of course was from *Titus* –

FELIX. You mean this was a *joke?!*

MADGE. Well, not a joke exactly –

GILLETTE. Not a joke at all! We're trying to find a murderer.

FELIX. Which means you *do* suspect one of *us!*

GILLETTE. Well not *exactly.*

AGGIE. I was frightened to death!

SIMON. I-I-I had my suspicions…

AGGIE. Oh you did not!

GILLETTE. *(to FELIX)* I'm sorry old man –

FELIX. Don't *touch* me, you idiot!

MADGE. Oh, darling –

FELIX. Don't *speak* to me!

GILLETTE. *(sternly)* Excuse me, but someone is trying to kill me, and I'd like to stop them before it's too late!

(They all start speaking at once:)

FELIX.	MARTHA.	SIMON.	AGGIE.	MADGE.
That is no excuse! You simply had no right to try and –	Willie, how could you! That was terribly thought-less –	I thought she was dead. Quite honestly I was frightened to –	I was scared to death! It was like reliving the entire *acci-dent*!	I'm sorry darling, I really am, I was simply trying to help –

*(Then everyone notices that **DARIA** is not joining in. She is standing apart from the others and she's white with rage. They all look at her and there's a beat of silence.)*

DARIA. …How dare you.

GILLETTE. Daria, I'm very sorry –

DARIA. *How dare you?!!* Is that all this *was* to you?! A parlor game?!

GILLETTE. Of course not –

DARIA. Am I a figure of *fun*?! Is that what you think of me?!

SIMON. Now wait a second. I had nothing to do with this –

DARIA. *Shut up!* You little worm. All you ever wanted was her money.

SIMON. *That is a lie! A dirty, filthy, stinking –*

MADGE. Simon!

DARIA. *(wheeling on* **MADGE***)* And you. Just look at you – and your two-bit actor husband. The man you adore. The man you would defend to the death. Has he told you yet that we slept together? That he made love to me in a New York hotel room?!

FELIX. …One night. Big mistake. No fun at all.

(Whap! **MADGE** *slaps* **FELIX** *hard across the face.)*

GILLETTE. Felix…

DARIA. *(to* **GILLETTE***)* And you, Mr. High and Mighty. The great William Gillette – just wait till I get through with *you* in my article. "Pompous man, pompous actor."

AGGIE. *Leave him alone!* You don't deserve to clean his shoes, you horrible –

DARIA. *Shut up!*

(to **GILLETTE***:)* Believe me, you will never work in the theatre again, let alone *star* in anything. People will laugh at you and your rude mother and your adoring girlfriend.

SIMON. *She's my wife!*

DARIA. And she's in love with *him!* Don't you see anything, you stupid fool! Now leave me alone! All of you! *Just get out of my sight!!*

MARTHA. This is my house!

DARIA. And I will be leaving it as soon as possible, but at the moment I would like some privacy.

(Everyone starts leaving the room. **SIMON** *hurries out, followed by* **AGGIE***:)*

AGGIE. Simon, you know it's not true. Simon!

*(***MADGE** *hurries out with* **FELIX** *pursuing her.)*

FELIX. It was just sex. It took five minutes. Three minutes. It went by so fast, I hardly remember it...

GILLETTE. Daria, I'm very sorry. I didn't mean to offend you.

DARIA. I will ruin you.

(And now they're all gone, and DARIA is alone. She paces, still crazed with rage, then grabs the telephone.)

DARIA. Hello...Operator?...*Operator?!*...Oh, good, I was afraid the line might be...Yes, yes, yes, just *listen* to me! Is there a local taxi company in this godforsaken place?...*I said is there a taxi*...T-A-X-I....*Well put them through.*...Ah, how do you do. Could you please send a taxi immediately to the Gillette House on Collins Lane....*Collins!*...*C-O-L-L* – that's right!...Yes, I'm sure it will be difficult to get through the snow, but that's your problem, now just *send me the goddam car!*

(She hangs up – and MARTHA enters holding a cup of tea.)

MARTHA. Hello?

DARIA. What do *you* want?

MARTHA. I thought you might like a cup of tea to help you calm down.

DARIA. I am perfectly calm, so please don't bother.

MARTHA. Oh it's no bother at all. And I'm sure that everyone feels sorry for hurting your feelings. It was entirely unintentional, you know.

DARIA. It was not unintentional at all. Your son knew exactly what he was doing, which was using the séance for his own ends!

MARTHA. But my son is in danger! Someone is trying to kill him! You will admit he has to do *something* about it.

DARIA. I admit no such thing, thank you very much. The police are handling the investigation, quite competently, I'm sure, and just because your son has neurotic delusions of being Sherlock Holmes is no reason to make the rest of us suffer.

MARTHA. He has no delusions at all!

DARIA. Oh, please. With his little gadgets and his laboratory and his railroad…Do you know, I think he's actually insane, no, really, insane, a madman, and should be *put away!*

MARTHA. *(seething)* How dare you say that?! How dare you!! It's *you* that should be put away! With your rudeness and your mediums and your séances.

DARIA. Oh shut up!

MARTHA. I knew girls like you when I was growing up. The bad girls, we called them. The malicious ones. They pretended they knew things because they were insecure.

DARIA. *Insecure?!*

MARTHA. They bullied people who were afraid of them. They spread rumors and lies because they were unpopular –

DARIA. *GET OUT, GET OUT, GET OUT OF MY SIGHT, YOU OLD HAG!!…*And just remember, I'm going to *ruin* your son. He'll be the laughingstock of the entire profession, *NOW LEAVE ME ALONE!!!*

*(**MARTHA** glares at her with fury, then marches out, still holding the teacup, shaking with rage. Almost immediately, there's a knock at the study door and **SIMON** comes in apologetically.)*

SIMON. Daria. I-I want to say again that I had nothing to do with that-that-that-that travesty. I mean I joked around, yes, and-and teased you a little, but you shouldn't blame *me* for that-that-that-

DARIA. Oh, stop blithering! I know what you're up to. You're scared to death! And you want everyone to think you're just an idiot –

SIMON. But I am just an idiot!

DARIA. Oh, get out.

SIMON. But Daria, please, this shouldn't affect anything else that we're –

DARIA. GET...OUT!

(He goes. Immediately **FELIX** *comes in.)*

FELIX. Don't speak. Ah! Don't! Not a word, just listen. As someone who was once your friend, *regardless* of our little mistake, I want you to know that this display of yours is entirely uncalled for and I suggest that you apologize to *everyone* before something untoward happens.

DARIA. "Untoward?"

FELIX. Un-expected. Un-fortunate. Now take my advice. You may not think that I'm your friend, but I am.

(He goes back up the stairs.)

DARIA. Felix? Felix, get down here! *Felix, I'm talking to you!!!*

(At which point **MARTHA** *reenters with the cup of tea. She marches up to* **DARIA** *and hands it to her.)*

MARTHA. I meant to leave this with you, but I took it with me by mistake.

*(***MARTHA** *walks out leaving* **DARIA** *alone.)*

DARIA. Is everyone in this house *insane?*

(BOOM! A bang of thunder, a flash of lightning, and the lights flicker on and off, remaining on but with less brightness. The thunder is so loud and frightening that it causes Portia to begin barking in the study.)

PORTIA. *Bark, bark, bark, bark, bark!*

*(***DARIA** *kicks the door open and yells:)*

DARIA. *Oh shut up!*

(She flings the contents of the tea cup at Portia, who howls and runs off. Then she flings the tea cup and saucer themselves, and they shatter off stage.)

*(***DARIA** *turns back to the room in fury. There is another loud boom of thunder and the lights in the room flicker on and off...then off for good.)*

Oh, dammit!

(The room is now in darkness and we can barely see **DARIA** *at all.)*

DARIA. *(cont.)* Stupid house, I can't see!...Hello?!...*Hello?! Where is everybody?!*

(No answer. We hear the wind outside. **DARIA** *starts to feel very nervous.)*

(Bump! A noise from the hallway.)

Hello?! Who is it?!

(Nothing. Then Bump!)

Hello...?

(We can see her outline in the darkness, but not much else. She sees someone in the hall and walks over.)

...Oh it's *you* again. Can't you people leave me alone?! Nag, nag, nag, you're all scared to de*AHHHHHHHH-HHHHHHHHHHHHHHHHHHHHHH!!!*

(The scream is heart-stopping. **DARIA** *has just been stabbed in the back with a very wicked-looking knife. She gasps and staggers from the door – at which moment the thunder booms, the lights flicker back on and we can see* **DARIA** *clearly now. Her face is contorted with pain and she staggers across the room, gasping and trying to get at the knife to pull it out.)*

Argh! Argh! Argh!

(After several seconds of this, she sees the phone and stumbles to it. She manages to pick it up and squawks into the receiver:)

Doctor! I need a doctor!...D-O-C...argh...

(She drops the phone and is trying to pick it up when **GILLETTE** *enters from the dining room.* **DARIA** *is facing him, so he can't see the knife.)*

GILLETTE. Ah, Daria, there you are. I bumped into Mother and she said that you called a taxi.

DARIA. Argh!

GILLETTE. Yes, I know you're angry, but I was hoping I could persuade you to stay.

DARIA. No. Help!

GILLETTE. Yes, I know the séance was no help, and it was very stupid of me. But you see I get these enthusiasms now and then and I just overdo it sometimes.

DARIA. *Knife in the back!*

GILLETTE. Yes, I'm sure it seemed like a knife in the back, but I was trying to catch a killer.

(She turns around to show him the knife in her back, but he happens to shake his head in self-deprecation and make a turn of his own at the same time.)

Sometimes I just want to *do* something, and not just entertain people…

(They both turn and face each other again.)

Now what do you say we forget the whole thing. Yes?

DARIA. *(Her body is moving spasmodically right and left).* Nargh, nargh!

GILLETTE. Well that's not very understanding, now is it?!

DARIA. *Nargh!*

GILLETTE. *All right, goodbye!*

(He storms out of the room. **DARIA** *is aghast. She staggers forward with her arms out.)*

DARIA. Back! Back!

(Suddenly, **GILLETTE** *marches back into the room and towards the kitchen.)*

GILLETTE. Oh, right, I forgot to lock the back door.

DARIA. Lock?…Don't lock. Look.

GILLETTE. I'm not *looking* at it. I'm *locking it.* I'm closing up for the night.

DARIA. *Look, look, LOOK!!*

GILLETTE. Daria, what in the devil are youahhhhhh.

DARIA. *AAAAAAAAAAAAAAAAAAAAAAAAAAAAAAAAAA AAAAAAAAARGHHHHH!*

(With a final scream, she collapses spectacularly onto the floor and dies. And now, at last, **GILLETTE** *sees the knife sticking out of her back.)*

GILLETTE. *Oh dear God.*

(He springs to her side and checks the pulse in her neck. He looks up in shock.)

She's…

(Thunder. Beethoven. Blackout.)

End of Act One

ACT TWO

Scene One

(The action is continuous. We hear the Beethoven quartet and then a huge crash of thunder and lightning. The wind howls and the snow is falling in sheets.)

*(When the lights come up, **GILLETTE** is still kneeling over **DARIA**'s body, taking her pulse, just as we left him.)*

GILLETTE. …dead!

*(A thousand thoughts are going through his brain, and his head darts from side to side, looking for a clue. This is a challenge worthy of **HOLMES** himself.)*

*(He looks carefully at the hilt of the knife sticking out of **DARIA**, then looks at the wall of weapons and sees the empty space where the knife used to hang.)*

Good God, it's my knife…

(He springs up and looks down the hall, then through the French doors and the door to the dining room. The killer is gone.)

*(He takes the afghan from the sofa and throws it over **DARIA**'s body, then he hurries to the telephone.)*

Hello, operator? Get me the police!…P-O-L-…yes, that's right, thank you…Hello? Is this the police? I have to report a murder.

*(At this moment, **MARTHA** enters from the hall.)*

MARTHA. Willie, dear –

GILLETTE. Mother, stay out of this room!

MARTHA. Oh, don't be ridiculous.

GILLETTE. Mother, please, there's something I don't want you to see.

(into the phone) Would you hold on a moment?

MARTHA. Who are you speaking with?

GILLETTE. The police actually. Now Mother listen. Brace yourself. This is going to be very upsetting, but Daria is dead.

MARTHA. Yes I know, dear. I killed her.

GILLETTE. ....What did you say?

MARTHA. I said I killed Daria.

GILLETTE. But she was murdered.

(He gestures up and down with his arm a few times, imitating the plunging of the knife.)

MARTHA. That was me, I'm afraid.

*(**MARTHA** starts to cry. She's extremely upset.)*

Oh, Willie!!

GILLETTE. *(into the phone)* I'll have to get back to you.

(He hangs up the phone.)

Mother, what happened?!

MARTHA. *(weeping)* Oh I was just so angry at Daria for speaking to you the way she did that I lost my temper!

GILLETTE. But mother, she was only threatening me.

MARTHA. Well, she'd have done it, too. She was ruthless. She was evil! *She was a theatre critic, for God's sake!*

(She weeps.)

I suppose I'll go to jail now, won't I.

GILLETTE. No. No, you won't. I won't let that happen, I promise you.

MARTHA. But how is that possible?

GILLETTE. I don't know yet, but you'll have to do everything I say.

MARTHA. I suppose I can try...

GILLETTE. Good. Now I want you to go upstairs and take one of your pills, it'll make you sleepy. No, take two.

MARTHA. When I take two I can't even see straight.

GILLETTE. Good, and then go to bed. We'll discuss it in the morning.

MARTHA. Oh, Willie, I'm so sorry for doing such a terrible thing, but I couldn't let her hurt you, I just couldn't.

GILLETTE. I understand. Now up you go. Straight to bed. You promised.

MARTHA. *(drying her tears)* Oh, all right. Nighty-night.

GILLETTE. Sleep tight.

MARTHA. Don't let the bed bugs bite.

(She hugs her son.)

Oh, Willie, I love you so much.

GILLETTE. And I love you.

MARTHA. Incidentally, that taxi Daria ordered before she died? I cancelled it. I took the view that she wouldn't need it once she was dead. Good-night, dear.

(She exits.)

GILLETTE. Oh my God…

(At this moment, FELIX appears at the top of the stairs and begins descending. He's angry and he doesn't look up – so he doesn't see the body at first.)

Oh, Felix, thank God. Come here, quickly.

FELIX. Don't speak to me, you reprobate.

GILLETTE. Yes, yes, I know, I was stupid, I apologize, I'm groveling, but I need your help!

FELIX. Oh I'm sure you do because you had to stage a séance, you had to pretend my wife was murdered, and you certainly had to what the hell is that?

*(**GILLETTE** lifts up the blanket a bit.)*

It's Daria.

GILLETTE. She's dead.

FELIX. …What's the joke?

GILLETTE. There is no joke. She's dead.

> (**FELIX** *chuckles appreciatively. He's sure this is a Gillette Special. He bends down and pokes the body.*)

FELIX. Badabadabada. Bidabidabida. Boodabooda*aaaaah! Oh my God! What happened?!*

GILLETTE. Knife to the back.

FELIX. Holy God! Who did this?!

GILLETTE. You're not going to believe it.

FELIX. Who?!

GILLETTE. Mother.

FELIX. My *mother* did this?

GILLETTE. Not *your* mother. *My* mother.

FELIX. Martha?

> (**GILLETTE** *nods.*)

Dear sweet Martha?

GILLETTE. She was furious because Daria threatened to ruin me. Now I need to protect her. Will you help me?

FELIX. Well of course I'll help you, she's like my own mother. But what are you thinking?

GILLETTE. I'm not sure. I suppose we should hide the body somewhere in the house. Then we'll claim that Daria left here right after the séance and we have *no idea at all where she was going.* Then, when things cool down, we'll get rid of the body.

FELIX. It does make us accessories to murder, you know.

GILLETTE. Well, if you don't want to help your dear sweet Martha who's been like a m –

FELIX. Oh shut up. We can't let her go to prison. Poor old thing, what kind of life has she had? She's been stuck with you for most of it....What are you doing?!

GILLETTE. Getting rid of the evidence.

> (**GILLETTE** *is kneeling over the body. He pulls the knife from* **DARIA***'s back, and it comes out with a hideous pop, spurting blood from the wound.*)

FELIX. Ah! Yuch!

(**GILLETTE** *whips a magnifying glass out of his pocket and examines the knife.*)

GILLETTE. Look at this. There are fingerprints all over it.

FELIX. You do know that you're not really Sherlock Holmes, don't you?

GILLETTE. (*preoccupied with his examination*) Of course I do, Watson.

(*BZZZZZ! The front doorbell.*)

Good God, who's that?!

FELIX. How should I know?! Maybe it's the *police* to arrest us for *murder.*

GILLETTE. That's very funny, ha, ha.

(*He hits the intercom button.*)

Hello, who is it?

VOICE THROUGH THE INTERCOM. (*a woman's voice, deep and ironic*) Good evening, this is the police.

(**GILLETTE** *lets out a yip and tries to turn it into a pleasant laugh.*)

To whom am I speaking, please?

GILLETTE. This is William Gillette, may I help you?

VOICE. Yes, I'd like to ask you a few questions. But it's rather snowy out here so may I come in, please?

GILLETTE. Certainly. Yes, I'll just be a moment, thank you *so* much.

(*He hits the switch, turning off the intercom. Then he notices the murder weapon in his other hand and he reacts with another yip. He puts the knife in the top drawer of the desk and slams it shut.*)

FELIX. Good God, what are the police doing here?!

GILLETTE. I just remembered. I called them after I found the body.

FELIX. Oh, great.

GILLETTE. But then Mother confessed and I told them not to come!

FELIX. Oh that's all right then.

(mimes holding a telephone)

"Hello, police? There's just been a murder but whoops I think my mother did it so please don't bother stopping by."

GILLETTE. Ho, ho, ho, I'm laughing behind this mask of horror on my face now *pick up the body so we can hide it!!*

(They pick up the body at the arms and legs and start dragging her from one end of the room to the other looking for a hiding place.)

FELIX. She's heavier than she looks!

GILLETTE. Well, put your back into it.

FELIX. She must weigh a thousand pounds.

GILLETTE. At least it was all in the right places.

FELIX. Where shall we put her?!

GILLETTE. What about the closet?

FELIX. Good idea.

(They get the closet door open.)

GILLETTE. Hoist her up!

FELIX. I'm trying! I don't think she fits.

GILLETTE. Let's stand her on end…That should do it… There.

FELIX. Good.

(They have her standing up in the closet, and **FELIX** *closes the door.)*

GILLETTE. I'll get the policeman.

(He heads for the door – but as he goes, the closet door swings open and the body starts to fall out.)

Felix!

FELIX. *Ah!*

*(***FELIX** *catches her.)*

GILLETTE. What are you doing?!

FELIX. It's not my fault!

GILLETTE. Of course it is, you didn't close the door properly!

(They get her back in the closet and close the door again.)

There! I'd better go.

*(**GILLETTE** hurries away – and the door swings open again and the body starts falling out…)*

Felix!

*(**FELIX** grabs the body and wrestles with it again.)*

FELIX. I didn't do anything!

*(Meanwhile, **GILLETTE** is trying to fix the lock on the closet door.)*

GILLETTE. It's the lock. It just won't catch.

FELIX. Who built this place, the three little pigs?!

*(BZZZZZ! **GILLETTE** rushes to the intercom again.)*

GILLETTE. Hello?!

VOICE. I'm getting very wet out here. I could make a snow angel if you'd like…

GILLETTE. Yes, no! I'm sorry, I'll be right there!

(He turns the intercom off.)

Wait! I have an idea.

(He pulls the lever on the bookshelf, and the recess with the bar in it swings into view.)

FELIX. Oh my God, that's perfect. Why didn't we start there?

GILLETTE. I forgot about it.

FELIX. *But it's your house!*

(They drag the body into the recess and get her onto a bar stool, slumped over the bar.)

GILLETTE. There. How's that?

FELIX. She looks like something out of Eugene O'Neill.

GILLETTE. You close up, I'll get the Inspector. Just push the handle.

(**GILLETTE** *hurries towards the hall.* **FELIX** *adjusts the body and hurries to the lever in the wall and pulls...but the recess doesn't close. He tries it again. Nothing moves. So the body is fully exposed and he can't close the door to the recess.*)

FELIX. Come on...would you close, you stupid...

(*He tries pulling on the door to the recess, but it won't move. By this time he hears voices in the hall.*)

GILLETTE. *(off)* Welcome, Inspector. Please come in.

INSPECTOR. *(off)* Thank you.

(*Panicked now,* **FELIX** *grabs the body and drags it behind the sofa, where it's hidden from view. Anyone walking behind the sofa, however, would see it instantly.*)

(*As he hides the body behind the sofa, the door to the recess moves into place by itself, hiding the bar.* **FELIX** *sees it close and watches with astonishment. Why is it closing now, when he wanted it to close earlier?! At this moment:*)

(**GILLETTE** *and* **INSPECTOR HARRIET GORING** *enter.* **INSPECTOR GORING** *is covered in snow. Goring is between 40 and 50 and she wears a tweed coat and a hat. She's British, eccentric, and one of a kind. One minute she seems wry and clever, the next minute she's off into a world of her own. She gets things wrong without even knowing it, yet she also seems just the sort of person who can find you out when you're lying. That makes her formidable.*)

(*She's also covered in snow at the moment and she isn't happy about it.*)

GILLETTE. I'm so sorry to keep you waiting, Inspector.

INSPECTOR. Not at all. I'm only sorry I forgot my snowshoes.

(During the following, **FELIX** *does his best to shield the back of the sofa. He also tries to draw* **GILLETTE***'s attention to the body, but* **GILLETTE** *just doesn't get it.)*

FELIX. Hello.

INSPECTOR. There is no means of escape, Professor Moriarty!

(She chuckles.)

I recognize you from Mr. Gillette's most interesting play.

FELIX. Oh. I see. Did you enjoy it?

INSPECTOR. I found it unlikely, illogical, far-fetched and I enjoyed it immensely. Especially when you plunged to your death.

FELIX. Thank you.

INSPECTOR. I've always liked Sherlock Holmes, of course. You can't be in my business and not appreciate him. He's such a misfit. I like misfits. I don't know why.

*(***GILLETTE** *and* **FELIX** *glance at each other. The* **INSPECTOR** *strolls around the room observing things.)*

FELIX. I don't suppose there's much crime out here in Connecticut, eh?

INSPECTOR. Oh, you'd be surprised. I have loads of cases, I just can't solve any of them. Ha! I seem to miss the clues for some reason. And yet I do catch all the criminals in the end. I don't know how exactly... *"The evil that men do lives after them! The good is oft interr'd with their bones!"* I thought I'd be an actress when I was a youngster, you see. I just never had the confidence, alas. But then I got a nose for blood, and that's all I needed. *"Blood will have blood!" "Is this a dagger which I see before me?!!"* No it isn't, actually, it's missing.

GILLETTE. I'm sorry?

INSPECTOR. The dagger from your wall. This spot here. I can see the discoloration from where the dagger used to be.

FELIX. You know, it is unusual meeting a *woman* detective. I didn't know they existed. Are you one of many?

INSPECTOR. Not yet, I'm afraid, but I believe you might call me the wave of the future. I think of myself as a pioneer, heading West, fertilizing the land as I go.

FELIX. I don't want to think too hard about that...

GILLETTE. So what can we do for you, Inspector?

INSPECTOR. Well, a few minutes ago, someone called the police station and reported a murder. According to the operator, the call came from this house.

FELIX. This house?

GILLETTE. That's ridiculous.

INSPECTOR. Then it wasn't either of you who called?

FELIX. No.

GILLETTE. Not at all.

INSPECTOR. I see. And how is your arm feeling?

GILLETTE. I beg your pardon?

INSPECTOR. The arm where you were shot two weeks ago on the stage of your theatre in New York City. It was in all the papers. You see, I believe that *if* these two events – the shooting and the call – are unrelated, then we've got ourselves quite a coincidence. And coincidence makes me *very* suspicious.

(Suddenly turning to **FELIX** *who has been trying to get* **GILLETTE** *to notice the dead body on the floor.)*

Do you have a twitch?

FELIX. Twitch? No. Yes. Why?

GILLETTE. Inspector, the fact is, nothing unpleasant has happened here tonight. Unless you count my rather poor singing voice during the Christmas carols. Ha ha!

FELIX. Ha ha!

GILLETTE. Ha ha ha!

FELIX. Ha ha ha!

(**GILLETTE** *now sees the body behind the sofa. If* **GILLETTE** *is still sitting opposite, perhaps* **FELIX** *lifts the leg of the cadaver behind the* **INSPECTOR***'s back.*)

GILLETTE. Hahahahaha*YAHHHHHAHAHAHAHA!*

INSPECTOR. Is something the matter?

GILLETTE. No, no. I-I-I just remembered a good joke.

INSPECTOR. Can you tell us?

GILLETTE. Well…there were these, uh, two Irishmen, and one says to the other, "Begorah, what's that dead body doin' on me livin' room floor." And the other one says –

FELIX. "Begorah, because the door to the bar wouldn't close!"

BOTH. *(desperately)* Hahahahahahaha!

(*The* **INSPECTOR** *looks bewildered.*)

INSPECTOR. Mr. Gillette, if you don't mind I'd like to take a look around for a moment. I'd like to jiggle your handles, as it were.

GILLETTE. Oh, absolutely. Feel free. Why don't you start in the kitchen. It's right through here, last door on the right.

INSPECTOR. Thanks so much, I'll just be a few minutes.

(*The* **INSPECTOR** *exits.* **GILLETTE**, *smiling, watches her go.*)

FELIX. *(smiling broadly through his teeth)* Is she gone yet?

GILLETTE. Not quite…*Yes, she's gone! Now why didn't you hide the body?!*

FELIX. That pull-thing of yours didn't work properly and I had to drag her out and then it closed all by itself!

GILLETTE. You didn't pull it properly.

FELIX. Of course I pulled it properly!

(*The* **INSPECTOR** *reenters unexpectedly – and the two men jump at the sound of her voice – and shield the back of the sofa.*)

INSPECTOR. Excuse me –

GILLETTE & FELIX. *Ahh!*

INSPECTOR. I forgot to ask, but is there anyone else staying here at the moment?

GILLETTE. Yes, indeed, we have Felix's wife, Madge. And Aggie and Simon, all from the play you saw, and of course my mother, who's very, *very* old and asleep upstairs, so if you could avoid disturbing her...

INSPECTOR. Of course, but I'd like to speak with the others if you don't mind.

GILLETTE. We'll call them down.

INSPECTOR. Thank you. I'll be in the kitchen.

(She exits again.)

GILLETTE. *(calling)* Help yourself to any of the leftovers.

INSPECTOR. *(off)* I intend to!

FELIX. *(smiling through his teeth again)* Is she gone *this* time?

GILLETTE. ....*Yes!*

FELIX. Thank God!

*(**GILLETTE** pulls the handle; the recess opens and they spring into action. Once again, they try to hide the body in the recess and close it to hide her.)*

FELIX. I've played a lot of supporting roles in my time, but this is ridiculous.

INSPECTOR. *(off) Mr. Gillette, may I ask you a question out here?*

GILLETTE. I don't believe it!

(calling) Yes, yes, just coming!

*(to **FELIX**)*

I'll be right back. And this time close it *with her inside!*

FELIX. Ooh, what a good idea. That's very helpful.

*(**GILLETTE** hurries off and **FELIX** manages to get the body over the bar again. His head is on the bar next to hers, trapped by her arm –)*

(when she raises her head and groans. She's not dead.)

(FELIX screams as the recess closes on both of them. FELIX is trapped inside the recess with the body.)

(A moment later, GILLETTE and the INSPECTOR enter from the dining room – and GILLETTE notices immediately that FELIX is nowhere to be seen.)

INSPECTOR. So then there are three exits to the grounds from this floor?

GILLETTE. Hm? Yes, no, four. Front door, French doors, kitchen door and the door to the library.

INSPECTOR. And where is the library exactly?

GILLETTE. Right through there.

INSPECTOR. Thank you so much.

(She starts to leave, then turns back.)

Order from chaos.

GILLETTE. I beg your pardon?

INSPECTOR. Order from chaos. That's what I do. Isn't it comforting?

(Chuckling happily, the INSPECTOR disappears down the hall, leaving GILLETTE alone in the room.)

GILLETTE. Felix?…*Felix?…*

(Tap…tap, tap…GILLETTE realizes that FELIX is inside the recess so he hurries to the handle and opens the door.)

Would you please stop fooling around!

FELIX. *She…she…she's still alive!!*

GILLETTE. Oh, don't be ridiculous.

FELIX. *She isn't dead yet! Just–just–just take her pulse or something.*

GILLETTE. Why don't you take it?

FELIX. *Because I'm not touching her!!*

(GILLETTE takes her pulse.)

Well?

GILLETTE. She's dead now.

FELIX. Oh, thank God! I mean I'm sorry, but –…

INSPECTOR. *(off)* *Mr. Gillette!*

FELIX. I'll go get the others and don't you ever, *ever* ask me to cover up a murder for you again.

(FELIX disappears up the stairs – and as soon as he's gone, the INSPECTOR reenters.)

INSPECTOR. Ah, Mr. Gillette. I just had a thought: Do you have any domestic help working here tonight?

GILLETTE. No, we don't. Our cook left after serving dinner, and I gave my butler the evening off. It is Christmas Eve, after all.

INSPECTOR. Is it? Of course it is. Merry Christmas. Now what about visitors? Did any of your neighbors drop in? Perhaps you had some carolers, eh? Deck the Halls, that sort of thing. I used to love visiting the neighbors on Christmas Eve. A bit of song, a bit of wassail, ha!, by the time we finished I could hardly stagger home!

GILLETTE. It sounds delightful, but I'm afraid it was just the cast and mother. A quiet evening with a few retiring friends.

(MADGE comes storming down the stairs followed by FELIX.)

MADGE. *Holy Hell in a Hand Basket!! This is just lovely, now a policeman wants to talk to me about a murder! Are you the policeman?!*

INSPECTOR. Police *woman*, actually.

MADGE. Good. Arrest my husband.

INSPECTOR. I beg your pardon.

MADGE. Arrest him! He's guilty as sin. And *of* sin as it happens. The charge is adultery.

FELIX. Madge, would you stop!

MADGE. Well, it's true, isn't it? You stood right here and admitted it in front of everybody!

FELIX. Well what was I supposed to do?!

MADGE. You could have lied like every other husband on the planet!

FELIX. Excuse me, but who's the one who pretended to be possessed tonight?! *"Look at me, I'm catatonic and I'm scaring my husband to death!"*

MADGE. *I did it to solve the mystery, didn't I?*

FELIX. *Well it didn't work, now did it!*

MADGE. *But it could have!*

FELIX. "Ladies and Gentlemen, the Academy Award this year goes to Madge Geisel for vomiting blood on her fellow guests this weekend."

(She slaps him across the face again.)

Ow!

(MADGE storms up the stairs. FELIX loses it and jumps up and down in frustration.)

FELIX. *MADGE GET BACK HERE, YOU'RE ACTING LIKE A LUNATIC!!!*

(He runs up the stairs after her and disappears. At which moment, AGGIE appears from the library eating a stalk of celery.)

AGGIE. What's going on? Was someone shouting?

GILLETTE. Aggie, I thought you were upstairs.

AGGIE. I came down to the kitchen for a snack.

INSPECTOR. Down?

AGGIE. The back stairs.

GILLETTE. Aggie Wheeler, Inspector Goring.

AGGIE. "Inspector?" Has something happened?

INSPECTOR. Well, we're not certain, but we believe there may have been a murder in this house.

AGGIE. A murder?! Oh no, who was murdered?!

INSPECTOR. That's the thing. We're not quite sure.

GILLETTE. Where's Simon?

AGGIE. I don't know. He seems to have…disappeared on me.

INSPECTOR. That's odd. When did you last see him?

AGGIE. I went upstairs earlier this evening, we all did, and

Simon gave me some wine and I fell asleep on the bed without even changing. I didn't know I was so tired, but I really conked out. It was like I was drugged or something...Anyway, when I woke up he was gone.

(There's a crash of thunder. The lights flicker and when they come back on, they're lower. Throughout this scene, the lights grow dimmer and the world becomes smaller and more threatening.)

*(**GILLETTE** goes to the intercom.)*

GILLETTE. *(his voice echoing through the house)* Simon? This is William. In whatever room you're in, could you go to the intercom and push the red button. It will open up the line between us...Simon?...Simon, can you hear me?...

(There is no answer. Just dead silence.)

AGGIE. *(getting very anxious)* William, tell me he's all right.

GILLETTE. I'm sure he's fine. You saw him just a half hour ago.

AGGIE. *He shouldn't have left me in the room!*

*(At this moment, **SIMON** enters from the dining room with a cookie and a glass of milk.)*

SIMON. What's going on? Is there a problem?

AGGIE. *(running to him and embracing him)* Oh, Simon!! Where have you been?!

SIMON. I was in the kitchen getting a snack.

INSPECTOR. How do you do. Inspector Goring, Middlesex County Police Department.

SIMON. Good heavens. Is something wrong?

AGGIE. There's been a murder.

SIMON. Oh my God.

GILLETTE. But not in this house.

INSPECTOR. You *think.*

GILLETTE. Well I believe I'd know if there was a murder in my own house.

FELIX. *(entering at the top of the stairs)* Where's Madge?

GILLETTE. What do you mean, "Where's Madge," she was with you.

FELIX. And then she huffed off and she's not in our room.

SIMON. She's probably in the bathroom.

FELIX. No, I looked and she wasn't there either!

SIMON. Why is everyone so jumpy all of a sudden?

AGGIE. I told you, there's a murderer on the loose!

(Boom! The storm is getting worse and worse. The lights flicker again and this time they come up even lower. **GILLETTE** *goes to his intercom again.)*

GILLETTE. Madge, if you can hear this would you…The line's dead.

INSPECTOR. What about the phones?…"Hello? Hello, operator…" Dead.

(A frisson of concern passes through the room. They all glance at each other.)

AGGIE. It's just the electricity…

FELIX. Except that Madge is missing!

INSPECTOR. This is thrilling!

GILLETTE. Felix, she was here five minutes ago.

FELIX. Excuse me, but I would know if my wife is missing or not and she is *definitely missing!*

(MADGE appears from the hallway eating an apple.)

MADGE. Who's missing?

FELIX. Oh thank God! Madge! Where have you been?!

MADGE. I was in the kitchen, getting a snack.

FELIX. You should have told me!

MADGE. That I was hungry?

INSPECTOR. Your kitchen seems to be very popular.

SIMON. Speaking of missing people, by the way, where's Martha?

GILLETTE. Upstairs asleep.

SIMON. Through all this?

GILLETTE. *Yes* through all this!

AGGIE. What about Daria?

INSPECTOR. Who's Daria?

MADGE. Daria Chase, the columnist.

INSPECTOR. She's staying here? At this house?

MADGE. Yes, that's right.

GILLETTE. She's not, actually.

FELIX. She left right after you all went to bed.

MADGE. In this weather?

GILLETTE. Well, she was upset, you know, and she simply insisted on walking out.

FELIX. That's right.

INSPECTOR. "Upset?"

GILLETTE. A little argument.

FELIX. It was nothing.

INSPECTOR. And did either of you *see* her leave?

GILLETTE. *(with a glance at* FELIX*)* Not exactly.

FELIX. But she said she was leaving.

AGGIE. Wait a second! That's her handbag!

(And now we notice it, in a corner of the couch.)

GILLETTE. She must have forgotten it.

FELIX. Women do.

MADGE. She'd never leave without her handbag. That's impossible.

FELIX. It's not *impossible!*

AGGIE. I agree with Madge. Women just don't.

INSPECTOR. Unless she was running from something.

AGGIE. Perhaps someone should look in her room.

MADGE. I'll go.

INSPECTOR. I'll go with you.

(They head up the stairs.)

SIMON. If I had killed Daria, I know where I'd have put her. In that hidden room of yours.

INSPECTOR. Hidden room?

GILLETTE. I don't *have* a hidden room, Simon.

SIMON. Oh you know what I mean, that bar thing. Martha showed us. You pull this handle.

FELIX. No, don't – !

GILLETTE. Don't do it – !

(Too late. **SIMON** *pulls the handle and the door to the recess slides open.)*

*(***GILLETTE** *and* **FELIX** *wince…but the recess is empty. There's no* **DARIA***.)*

*(***GILLETTE** *and* **FELIX** *look at each other, puzzled.* **AGGIE** *goes into the recess and stands in front of the bar.)*

AGGIE. I don't know what you two are thinking, but there's nothing h –

(At which moment, **DARIA***'s arm and then her whole body shoot out from behind the bar and she grabs* **AGGIE** *with a horrible gasp.)*

DARIA. *Ahhhhhhhhhhhhhhhhhh!*

AGGIE. *(terrified) AHHHHHHHHHHHHHHHHHHHHH HHHHHHHHHHHHHH!*

*(***AGGIE** *screams and screams.)*

(Thunder and lightning.)

(Blackout)

End of Scene

Scene Two

(About five minutes later. Daria's body is gone. **AGGIE** *is weeping in* **SIMON**'s *arms, the* **INSPECTOR** *is pacing, extremely cross, and* **MADGE** *is standing apart.)*

MADGE. ...I guess this means we're not exchanging presents tonight...

*(**AGGIE** continues weeping.)*

SIMON. Shhh. It's all right, it's over now.

INSPECTOR. I'm afraid it isn't over, Mr. Bright. Miss Chase has been murdered and I have been lied to.

*(**FELIX** and **GILLETTE** enter together, a little winded, rolling their sleeves down, etc.)*

MADGE. Did you dispose of the body as they do in the mysteries?

FELIX. We put her in the greenhouse next to a very beautiful orchid. She looks rather holy.

MADGE. Well that's a first.

GILLETTE. *(to the* **INSPECTOR**, *who is glowering at him)* You're still cross with me, aren't you?

INSPECTOR. You could have told me about the séance, and you could have told me about Mr. Boggs.

GILLETTE, SIMON, FELIX. Noggs.

INSPECTOR. Well whoever he was! The man was murdered last night and you don't even tell me about it?!

GILLETTE. I'm awfully sorry, I was going to say something, but then –

INSPECTOR. Oh stop it! You were shot two weeks ago, Mr. Gillette, and if I were in your stockings I'd feel rather concerned at the moment.

FELIX. Do you really think there's a connection with all this?

INSPECTOR. Well, of course there is! There has to be! We just can't see it yet because we're *in the forest*.

(Boom!)

INSPECTOR. *(cont.)* Now I'll need some assistance, but I assume that this telephone is still dead.

(She picks up the receiver.)

"Hello...Hello!"

(It's obviously dead. She hangs it up.)

And I suppose no one knows where the murder weapon is?

(No answer. Everyone shrugs.)

All right, I would like all of you to go into the dining room and wait for me, and I urge you to keep an eye on each other. No one leaves! I'll call you for questioning one at a time, and believe me, this is not a joke.

(Everyone exits except **GILLETTE**, *who closes the door behind them.)*

GILLETTE. Good. Let's get down to business. I fear it's more complicated than I thought at first. They all have motives.

INSPECTOR. What are you talking about? Get in there!

GILLETTE. Surely *I'm* not a suspect.

INSPECTOR. Of course you are.

GILLETTE. But it's my house.

INSPECTOR. What has that got to do with it? If anything, it means you're a bigger suspect. You know the house inside-out and you knew about the hidden room.

GILLETTE. You know, when you think about it, you're just as much a suspect as I am.

INSPECTOR. I beg your pardon.

GILLETTE. It happens all the time in murder mysteries. The slightly odd "inspector" who arrives alone in the middle of the night and pretends to sort things out when in fact she intends to murder someone for some hideous crime that happened twenty years ago.

INSPECTOR. Oh nonsense.

GILLETTE. I don't see a badge.

INSPECTOR. I left it at the office.

GILLETTE. That's a likely story.

INSPECTOR. *You hid a murder and you're accusing me of stories?!*

(**MARTHA** *walks in wearing her dressing gown. She is rather loopy from her sleeping pills.*)

MARTHA. Hello...?

GILLETTE. *(alarmed)* Mother, what are you doing here?!

MARTHA. I heard a scream and it woke me up. At least I think it was a scream. It might have been a tea kettle.

GILLETTE. Mother, go back to bed. Right now.

MARTHA. Oh don't be silly. I am perfectly fine. How do you do. Are you a stranger?

INSPECTOR. Yes I am, I'm afraid.

MARTHA. Oh that's all right. I like strange men, don't I, Willie. Sometimes. If they're nice. Are you nice?

INSPECTOR. I like to think so.

GILLETTE. Mother, how many sleeping pills did you take?

(Embarrassed, **MARTHA** *holds up four fingers.)*

MARTHA. *(confidentially to the* **INSPECTOR***)* They make me sleepy.

GILLETTE. All right, back to bed.

MARTHA. Oh, stop it!

(to the **INSPECTOR***)* How do you do, I'm Martha Gillette.

INSPECTOR. How do you do. Inspector Goring from the Middlesex County Police Department.

MARTHA. *Oh, no!*

GILLETTE. Mother –!

MARTHA. I knew it would come to this, I just knew it.

INSPECTOR. So you know about the murder then?

MARTHA. Of course I know. How could I not know it when I was the one who –

GILLETTE. *Mother!* Don't say anything. Not a word!

MARTHA. Oh stop it. We knew it would come to this and I want to get it over with. *"It is a far, far better thing I do than I have ever done before. It is a far, far better place I go – "*

GILLETTE. Inspector, listen to me! I didn't want my mother to hear this, but…I killed Daria Chase. I'm turning myself in.

MARTHA. Willie!

INSPECTOR. Good God! Are you serious?

GILLETTE. Yes. She threatened to ruin my career and I couldn't just stand by and let her do it.

MARTHA. *(overlapping)* Oh stop being nonsensical. Inspector, I killed Daria Chase and he's trying to protect me.

GILLETTE. *(overlapping)* Mother, please. The Inspector can *see* that you couldn't do it. You're…you're too old.

MARTHA. Come over here and say that and I'll knock you down!

INSPECTOR. *Would you both be quiet!*

(**MARTHA** *breaks down in tears.*)

MARTHA. *Oh, Willie, how could I do such a thing!* And I didn't *mean* to kill her! She just made me *so angry!*

(She sobs in his arms. **GILLETTE** *looks up. There's something wrong here.)*

GILLETTE. ……You didn't "mean to"?

MARTHA. I only wanted to make her sick and teach her a lesson!

(**GILLETTE** *pulls his mother aside and whispers to her:)*

GILLETTE. Excuse us…Mother, you must have realized it would kill her.

MARTHA. No I didn't! I thought, "You can't treat my son that way! I'll make you suffer first. I'll make you sick as a dog!"

GILLETTE. But you stabbed her in the back!

MARTHA. What are you talking about? How could I stab anybody?

GILLETTE. You used the knife from the wall and then you… oh my God you didn't kill her.

MARTHA. I didn't?

GILLETTE. Mother, what did you say a moment ago about getting sick or something…?

MARTHA. I said I'd make her sick as a dog, the way she threatened you and –

GILLETTE. *(overlapping) That's it! That's it!*

MARTHA. But what is that supposed to –

GILLETTE. Be quiet! Listen!

MARTHA. …Willie –

GILLETTE. *Listen!*

(They strain to listen. The **INSPECTOR,** *who has over-heard everything, is listening too.)*

MARTHA. I don't hear a thing.

INSPECTOR. Neither do I.

GILLETTE. It's the case of the dog in the night.

MARTHA. But I don't hear a dog.

GILLETTE. *(joyously) Exactly!* Mother, quick! Go find Portia!

MARTHA. What has Portia got to do with it?

GILLETTE. She may be ill, or she may be…Oh, quickly, Mother, go find her!

*(***MARTHA** *hurries off.)*

Inspector, listen. I retract my confession *and* my mother's. We didn't do it.

INSPECTOR. But I heard her confess!

GILLETTE. But she didn't mean it and that's the point.
*"She's as innocent as the new-born lamb
A-feeding on the crest of yonder hill."*

INSPECTOR. *Othello?*

GILLETTE. I just made it up.

*(***MARTHA** *reenters, carrying the dog in her arms. Poor Portia is limp and ill. The crisis has made* **MARTHA** *more level-headed.)*

GILLETTE. How's Portia?

MARTHA. She's very ill. I should have realized that wicked woman might do such a thing.

INSPECTOR. Do what thing? What are you talking about?!

GILLETTE. Look, it's simple. My mother was angry with Daria for threatening me, so to teach her a lesson she gave her – what? A cup of tea?

MARTHA. Yes.

GILLETTE. With something in it to make her sick.

MARTHA. Yes. Well not at first. First I brought her a regular cup, but when she became abusive I went back and doctored it.

GILLETTE. With one of the chemicals I left in the kitchen.

MARTHA. It said on the bottle "if ingested, causes violent stomach pains," and I thought, "Well, that's just the thing."

GILLETTE. But she didn't drink the tea, she must have thrown it at Portia, who licked it off the floor.

MARTHA. That's it, that makes sense! But I must get Portia to bed right away good-bye.

(**MARTHA** *hurries off with Portia in her arms.*)

GILLETTE. Mother, wait! Earlier, when I went:

(*He does the stabbing gesture again, his arm moving up and down from the elbow.*)

and you nodded, what did you think I meant?

MARTHA. I thought you were cheering me on about the poison.

(*She makes the gesture.*)

"Go, Mother! Go, Mother!" I'll see you later.

(*She hurries out of the room with Portia.*)

GILLETTE. *(exuberant; at the top of his game)* Ha ha! We're back in business! And now we have a murderer to catch!

INSPECTOR. "We?"

(GILLETTE goes to his mantelpiece and takes up his meerschaum pipe, then starts pulling on a Holmes-like dressing gown.)

GILLETTE. Now let's review what we know so far: we know that Daria must have been murdered in the fifteen minutes after the séance because that's when I came in and found her. So that puts the murder between 8:45 and 9 pm.

*(By this time, **GILLETTE** is smoking the meerschaum and has fastened the dressing gown. He's now the very picture of Sherlock Holmes.)*

INSPECTOR. *Mr. Gillette!* Let me remind you that *I* am in charge of this case, and you are by no means ruled out as a suspect.

GILLETTE. A: I'm not a suspect and you know it, B: You do need my help since I know everyone involved, and C: I haven't ruled *you* out as a suspect, and in fact you seem rather odd to me. Now who shall we start with?

INSPECTOR. Call Aggie and Simon in. And no funny business!

GILLETTE. *(opens the door)* Aggie, Simon, could you step in, please. I need to ask you some questions. The Inspector will take notes for me.

INSPECTOR. *I do not find that even faintly amusing!* This is *my case*, and it shall *remain* that way!

*(to **AGGIE** and **SIMON**, who are just entering:)* Now both of you sit down. I want to discuss your relationship with Daria Chase. How did you know her?

AGGIE. I only met her this evening.

SIMON. I met her at Killington, the ski resort.

INSPECTOR. And when was this?

SIMON. Just over a year ago.

INSPECTOR. And how did you meet?

SIMON. She recognized me from a play I was in. She'd given me a bad review about a swimsuit.

INSPECTOR. "Swimsuit?"

SIMON. I wore a swimsuit in the play and she implied that it was…too loose.

INSPECTOR. Loose? But how could she tell if it was…Oh. Sorry.

SIMON. Anyway, I'd never even been to Killington before and there she was. I think she goes there pretty often as a sort of getaway.

INSPECTOR. And why were you there?

AGGIE. He was helping me.

INSPECTOR. Helping?

AGGIE. I was on my honeymoon and my husband Hugo was killed in a skiing accident.

INSPECTOR. I read about that! He was a big wheel. Oh my Lord! I'm so sorry!

AGGIE. Thank you. After it happened I called Simon to help me deal with it.

GILLETTE. And you got there overnight.

SIMON. Yes, I borrowed a friend's car and drove for about seven hours.

INSPECTOR. *(taking notes)* I see. And the name of your friend who owned the car, please?

(**SIMON** *glances uncomfortably at* **AGGIE**.)

AGGIE. Tamsin McGregor.

SIMON. Yes.

AGGIE. That was his girlfriend at the time.

INSPECTOR. I see.

AGGIE. Simon, you can talk about it, it's fine.

(*to the* **INSPECTOR** *and* **GILLETTE**) She still calls him, apparently. She doesn't want to give him up.

SIMON. *(to* **AGGIE**) I asked her to stop calling.

AGGIE. I know that.

SIMON. I even told Mr. Gillette about it.

GILLETTE. That's right. She called this afternoon and I answered the phone. She sounded upset, I'm afraid.

SIMON. I'm sorry you had to be involved.

GILLETTE. Oh not at all. But the one thing I don't understand is how she got my telephone number.

SIMON. I guess she looked it up, or called the operator.

GILLETTE. That's not possible. It's unlisted.

SIMON. ...Well I don't know. Maybe she saw it in my address book.

GILLETTE. While you were still a couple?

SIMON. Right.

GILLETTE. Except that was, what? – almost a year ago?

SIMON. That's right.

GILLETTE. And I moved into this house just three months ago. So there was no telephone number a year ago. It didn't exist.

SIMON. *(getting upset)* Well, I don't know. Maybe she got it from a friend of yours, or your agent or something. I mean, she knew I was coming here, I told her *that,* but I also told her not to call under any circumstances! I begged her. I said *don't call!*

(Brring! The telephone rings. Everyone looks at it.)

(Brring!)

INSPECTOR. ...The telephone seems to be working again.

(Brring! **GILLETTE** *picks it up.)*

GILLETTE. Hello?

(He listens; then offers the phone to **SIMON***:)*

Tamsin.

*(***SIMON** *takes the phone.)*

SIMON. Hello?...No. But Tamsin, how did you get this number?...Tell me....Because I need to know!...Look, just calm down, I'm not accusing you of anything....*Calm down!*...Tamsin, yes of course I...

(He looks at **AGGIE** *and lowers his voice.)*

SIMON. *(cont.)* I did *at the time.* But things change. I'm sorry.

> (**AGGIE** *hurries out of the room.*)

Oh, God. Aggie! Wait!…Tamsin, I have to go, I'm sorry. *Yes, I'll call you back!*

> (*He hangs up. To the* **INSPECTOR***:*)

May I…?

> (*The* **INSPECTOR** *nods and* **SIMON** *hurries out of the room, leaving* **GILLETTE** *and the* **INSPECTOR** *by themselves. Beat.*)

INSPECTOR. "The silence between the two professionals spoke volumes."

> (**GILLETTE** *doesn't respond. He's thinking.*)

It's too bad we can't find the murder weapon. It's one of the many things I find odd about this case. It could have fingerprints on it, it could be broken in some way, or wiped clean or any one of a –

GILLETTE. Inspector, would you please stop babbling about useless details, I need to think.

INSPECTOR. I would hardly call the murder weapon a "useless detail," Mr. Holmes. It could tell us everything.

GILLETTE. It won't. I've already inspected it.

INSPECTOR. *What?*

GILLETTE. It's in the drawer.

> (*The* **INSPECTOR** *rushes to the drawer, opens it and pulls out the knife.*)

INSPECTOR. Good God! *Why didn't you tell me?!…Mr. Gillette!*

GILLETTE. Inspector, I have no idea why I didn't tell you, but now you've found it so would you *please be quiet BECAUSE I'M TRYING TO THINK!*

> (*At which moment,* **FELIX** *bursts into the room followed by* **MADGE.***)*
>
> (*They're both buoyant, at the top of their game.*)

MADGE. We've got it!

FELIX. We've got it!

MADGE. We know whodunit.

FELIX. What a team we are.

MADGE. Like Astaire and Rogers.

FELIX. Nick and Nora.

MADGE. Sacco and Vanzetti.

FELIX. You know, we *could* do this professionally.

MADGE. We're awfully good at it.

INSPECTOR. What are you talking about?!

FELIX. We've solved the murder.

MADGE. It's all wrapped up.

FELIX. Don't try to thank us.

INSPECTOR. But you are suspects yourselves!

MADGE. Not anymore. We figured it out.

FELIX. You may call the Sheriff and clean up this town.

GILLETTE. What's your guess?

FELIX. It isn't a guess at all. Look, let's start with a proposition: whoever murdered Daria is behind the whole thing. All right? All the murders and the attempted murder.

MADGE. Working backwards, that includes Daria, Noggs, you and Hugo.

INSPECTOR. I thought Hugo was an accident.

FELIX. Oh, puh-lease. "Coincidence?"

INSPECTOR. Fair enough. Go on.

FELIX. So who are the suspects. The people in this house, right?

MADGE. Ussens.

FELIX. But.

MADGE. But!

FELIX. Process of elimination. First we eliminate Martha. Fair?

INSPECTOR. Well…

MADGE. Can you really see her killing Hugo?

FELIX. Or hiring someone to shoot at her son?

MADGE. Then killing Noggs?

FELIX. With a razor blade?

INSPECTOR. All right, I give.

MADGE. *(to GILLETTE)* Now what about you. Did *you* do it?

GILLETTE. Oh please.

FELIX. *(to the INSPECTOR)* And you?

INSPECTOR. Don't be ridiculous!

FELIX. So now we're down to four suspects. Let's start with us. Did you do it, darling?

MADGE. No, my love. And you?

FELIX. Not a chance.

INSPECTOR. But those are denials! They carry no weight whatsoever!

FELIX. Except

MADGE. Except

FELIX. For Noggs.

MADGE. Good old Noggsy.

GILLETTE. What about him?

FELIX. He was killed last night, and we were staying at my sister's house in Rhinebeck last night.

MADGE. We have ten witnesses.

(silence)

GILLETTE. I see it all.

FELIX. I thought you would.

INSPECTOR. *What?*

FELIX. We're down to Aggie and Simon…*and Simon lied*!

INSPECTOR. When?

FELIX. He and Daria met at Killington. They both said so. But she said she left there *before* Hugo died,

MADGE. and *he* said he arrived there *after the killing* – in response to Aggie's call for help.

INSPECTOR. But why should Simon lie about when he arrived at Killington?

GILLETTE. So he could murder Hugo and get away with it!

FELIX/MADGE. Bingo.

INSPECTOR. But why on earth would he murder Hugo?

GILLETTE. The money! Don't you see it? Simon arrives at Killington on let's say Saturday and he plans the murder. Then he *pretends* to arrive on Tuesday so he can play the hero with Aggie, and it works because later he marries Aggie and as her husband gets half the money.

FELIX. And Daria knew all this because she happened to be at Killington and saw him –

MADGE. So she became a threat to Simon and he had to kill her.

FELIX. Case closed.

INSPECTOR. Wait! Mr. Gillette got shot at the Palace Theater. How does *that* fit in? Admittedly, Simon could have hired someone, but why shoot *you?* He was already married to Aggie – it doesn't make sense.

FELIX. I have an idea about that.

GILLETTE. So do I.

MADGE. So do I! He missed, right?

INSPECTOR. Well of course he missed. He hit Mr. Gillette's arm. Though from that distance I'd have put it right through his heart, let it ricochet twice around the theater and have it come back between his testicles.

*(***GILLETTE*** *and* ***FELIX*** *cross their legs.)*

MADGE. You don't understand. This man missed entirely. He was shooting at *Aggie*, he missed her, and the bullet hit *Willie.*

INSPECTOR. Ingenious! But why on earth was he shooting at Aggie?

ALL THREE. *Tamsin.*

INSPECTOR. Tamsin?

MADGE. Simon has a girlfriend!

FELIX. And he's in love with her!

GILLETTE. Just look at it from Simon's point of view. He kills Hugo and marries Aggie to get her money, but he's not in love with Aggie, he's in love with Tamsin. Solution:

GILLETTE/FELIX/MADGE/INSPECTOR. Kill Aggie.

INSPECTOR. And Tamsin has your telephone number because Simon gave it to her.

GILLETTE. *(simultaneously) gave it to her!*

MADGE. So if I may, a recap, from the beginning, just once.

FELIX. Go.

MADGE. Simon is in love with Tamsin and he's friends with Aggie.

FELIX. Then Aggie marries Hugo, who is rich as Croesus.

GILLETTE. So Simon, who is ambitious,

MADGE. And a sociopath,

INSPECTOR. Kills Hugo, marries Aggie, gets the money, and decides to kill Aggie so he and Tamsin can enjoy the loot.

FELIX. So he leaves a note making it look like Gillette was the intended victim.

MADGE. But.

FELIX. But! Noggs overhears Simon hiring someone to shoot Aggie,

MADGE. And whoever it is, misses Aggie, his intended victim, and hits our beloved leader here.

GILLETTE. And meanwhile, Simon kills Noggs because he's heard something.

INSPECTOR. On top of which, Daria knows the truth because of Killington

FELIX. And blackmails Simon,

MADGE. So he stabs her in the back!

FELIX. …Well, that's simple enough.

GILLETTE. It is, actually. It's like *Richard the Third*. Ruthless man kills everyone he needs to in order to get what he wants. The rest is detail.

(At which moment, **MARTHA** *enters from the dining room.)*

MARTHA. Hello, my dears.

GILLETTE. Mother, how's Portia?

MARTHA. She's going to be fine, thank God.

MADGE. Martha, have you seen Simon around?

MARTHA. Well, yes I have, actually. I was in the kitchen, and I saw him outside walking to the boathouse. In this weather! That's ridiculous.

FELIX. A getaway?

INSPECTOR. Possibly.

MADGE. Wait a second – was Aggie with him?

MARTHA. I couldn't see very well, but I think she might have been.

MADGE. Oh God.

GILLETTE. She's still in danger. I wasn't *thinking*.

FELIX. But he wouldn't do anything to her *here*, would he?

INSPECTOR. Who knows what he'd do. He's getting desperate.

GILLETTE. You go out the French doors and surround them!

(They rush to the French doors.)

MADGE. Wait! I think we should make lots of noise so he knows we're coming and thinks twice about hurting her.

INSPECTOR. That's excellent!

MADGE. *Ayeyeyeyeyeyeyeye!*

FELIX. *Ayeyeyeyeyeyeyeye!*

ALL FOUR. *AYEYEYEYEYEYEYEYE!*

(And they run out, leaving **MARTHA** *alone looking completely bewildered.)*

MARTHA. The word "madhouse" doesn't begin to describe it.

(She exits up the stairs, leaving the room empty.)

(Thunder. The wind howls.)

(pause)

(stillness)

(Then **AGGIE** *enters from the study.)*

AGGIE. …Hello?…Where is everybody?

(She walks to the hall and opens the door. There's a flash of lightning and we see **SIMON** *through the French windows behind her looking into the room.)*

Hello?!…William?!…

*(***SIMON** *enters the room quietly. Then* **AGGIE** *turns.)*

Oh! You startled me.

SIMON. Sorry.

(He stares at her.)

AGGIE. Where have you been? What's the matter with you?

SIMON. Nothing.

(silence)

AGGIE. Do you want to call Tamsin back. Is that it?

SIMON. You know that's not true.

AGGIE. Do I? You sounded pretty friendly on the phone just now.

SIMON. I didn't mean to.

AGGIE. Oh, Simon. Are you still in love with her? Tell me the truth! Please!

SIMON. No.

AGGIE. No what? That you're not in love with her, or not telling me the truth?

SIMON. …What do you think?

(Beat. Then they laugh uneasily.)

AGGIE. I'm sorry, I just…I get so jealous sometimes. I was looking for you and I couldn't find you.

SIMON. I went outside to do some thinking. What a weekend. Can I get you a drink?

AGGIE. I'd love one.

SIMON. Have a seat. It'll just take a minute.

(She starts to sit.)

No, no. Sit here. You can see outside. The light is so beautiful.

(He offers her a chair so she can't see the wall of weapons behind her. She sits. SIMON stares at the back of her head for a moment, then takes down a garrote. Thunder, and the lights dim.)

*(**AGGIE** leans her head back and takes a deep breath.)*

AGGIE. Oh. I'm so tired.

SIMON. Are you...?

AGGIE. Oh, my neck! Could you massage it?

SIMON. Of course.

(He puts down the garrote and begins massaging her neck.)

How's that?

AGGIE. Heaven.

(He works on her neck in silence for a moment. She sighs deeply.)

Wouldn't it be wonderful to live in a place like this?

SIMON. You *can* afford it, you know.

AGGIE. That's true. But I meant this kind of life. Like the Inspector.

(He continues to massage her neck... and then his fingers go around her throat...)

I could solve all the local mysteries and put things right again. I love that sort of tidiness, when all the pieces fit so perfectly together and everything just locks into place. That's when they catch the *really* bad people. "Where did the Pennyfeather's cat disappear to?" She's on the roof. "Who dug up Miss Pilbeam's flower bed last night?" It was that darn dog again. "Why do the Wheelers beat their daughter every night? She tries so hard to be perfect."

SIMON. I know you do.

   (pause)

AGGIE. We had the perfect plan, didn't we.

SIMON. We did.

AGGIE. I marry Hugo. I get the money. We kill Hugo. We get married.

SIMON. Then Daria had to come along and stick her nose in it. Out of the blue!

   (Agitated, **SIMON** *walks to the bar and starts making a drink.* **AGGIE** *stands.)*

AGGIE. She was on to you like a shot.

SIMON. The stupid cow. I always hated her. Do you know she tried to blackmail me. *Me!*

AGGIE. Is that why you killed her?

SIMON. No. I didn't kill her. That's the funny thing. It wasn't me.

AGGIE. Oh, really? And yet, on the other hand, you tried to kill me, didn't you?

   *(***SIMON*** looks at her, startled – and* **AGGIE** *snatches up the garrote and whips it over* **SIMON***'s head and starts to strangle him without mercy. She's pulling so hard, he can barely claw at his neck. Meanwhile, the storm outside is raging.)*

   You hired that man to shoot at me in the theatre, didn't you?! DIDN'T YOU?!

SIMON. *(strangling)* Yes!

AGGIE. *And you were about to try it again, weren't you?!*

SIMON. Arghh…Aggie, please!

AGGIE. Aggie please *what?!* Leave you and Tamsin to enjoy my money?!

SIMON. No!

AGGIE. *Liar! Admit it!*

SIMON. *Argh!*

AGGIE. *You're still in love with her, aren't you?! ADMIT IT OR I'LL KILL YOU!!*

(Beat. He shakes his head yes – and Snap! She gives the garrote a final yank and **SIMON***'s body goes limp and he falls to the floor.* **AGGIE** *undoes the garrote, and is catching her breath, when she hears voices outside.)*

INSPECTOR. *(off)* I'll go round the front!

MADGE. *(off)* We'll take the lawn!

GILLETTE. *(off)* I'll try the house!

*(***AGGIE** *runs to the French windows to look out – when suddenly* **SIMON** *begins to stir.)*

SIMON. Unhhh…

*(***AGGIE** *turns, shocked. She looks around desperately, grabs a heavy bronze statuette from a table and races to him. As he begins to get to his knees, she smashes him in the head with a horrible thud and he collapses to the floor again and doesn't move.)*

GILLETTE. *(off) Aggie?!*

(Panting, **AGGIE** *springs into action. She tousles her hair and rips her dress – clearly she's planning to pretend that she's just been attacked. She strikes a pose and is about to start wailing, when* **SIMON** *starts moaning again.)*

SIMON. Unnhhhh!

*(***AGGIE** *is dumbfounded.* **SIMON** *tries to get to his feet.)*

AGGIE. *Would you stop it!*

*(***AGGIE** *runs to the wall and grabs a shotgun. She's about to shoot him – but decides instead to club him with it. Wham!* **SIMON** *hits the floor, dead at last – and* **AGGIE** *starts wailing just as* **GILLETTE** *runs in the door.)*

GILLETTE. *Aggie!*

AGGIE. *Oh, William! William! Oh, thank God!* He tried to kill me! And he killed Hugo! He admitted it! And he put this horrible thing round my neck and I managed to squirm out of it and I got it around *his* neck and I…*I could hardly breathe!*

(AGGIE bursts into racking sobs and flings herself at GILLETTE.)

AGGIE. It was Simon all along! He still loved Tamsin! That's what he said! Oh, William, I love you so much!

(She clings to him for dear life.)

And we can find our love again, I promise. *I promise.*

GILLETTE. Oh my darling, that's wonderful! And may I tell you something?

AGGIE. Of course you can. You can tell me anything in the world!

GILLETTE. I turned the tape recorder back on before I ran outside.

(He takes the remote control device out of his pocket and holds it up. AGGIE's eyes widen in terror.)

AGGIE. No! No, don't!...*Don't play it! Please! Please!!*

(He's about to hit the button...but doesn't.)

GILLETTE. I didn't put it together until I was outside. You married Simon because you had to. He helped you kill Hugo because that was the way to get the money.

(AGGIE bolts to the wall and grabs a pistol.)

AGGIE. Get back! Get back! I'll shoot, I swear to God!

(She aims the gun at his head.)

GILLETTE. Aggie.

AGGIE. *You didn't love me enough, did you?! I wasn't good enough for you, the great William Gillette! Well I didn't need you! I found Hugo!!*

GILLETTE. Aggie, please.

(She fires! Click.)

GILLETTE. You don't think I leave them around loaded, do you?

(With a cry of frustration, AGGIE throws the pistol down and races to the hall, fleeing for her life – and runs straight into the INSPECTOR, who's waiting for her. Simultaneously, FELIX and MADGE reenter.)

INSPECTOR. No you don't!

AGGIE. *Ah! Let me go! Let go of me!*

> *(She's struggling so hard that the* **INSPECTOR** *can't hold her.)*

INSPECTOR. *Mr. Geisel! Would you help me here!* My God, Mr. Gillette, you were right! She's a wildcat!

> *(***FELIX** *helps hold on to her.)*

AGGIE. *Stop it! Stop it! I hate you!*

> *(Amid cries and grunts, they finally subdue her and handcuff her. By the end, she's panting like a trapped animal, exhausted.)*

If you hadn't recorded me with that stupid machine I'd have gotten away with it!

GILLETTE. I hate to tell you this, but I didn't put the machine on. That was a bluff.

AGGIE. AHHHH!

FELIX. Aggie. Why?

AGGIE. "Why?" How's fifty million dollars "why." How's getting to dress perfectly and act perfectly and get treated perfectly. *EXCEPT SIMON HAD TO GO AND RUIN IT, THE LYING, WOMANIZING LITTLE CHEAT!*

> *(She kicks the body – and* **SIMON** *starts upward with a gasp. They all jump back, and* **SIMON** *gets to his knees.)*

SIMON. Unnnhhhh…What happened?…

> *(He looks up and sees everyone staring at him.)*

Uh oh.

INSPECTOR. Mr. Bright, you are under arrest for the attempted murder of Miss Agatha Wheeler, the murder of her husband, Hugo, and the murder of Miss Daria Chase. If you would like to make a statement –

SIMON. Hey, wait a second! I didn't kill Daria. *She* did!

AGGIE. *Liar!* Why would I murder Daria?! It was your alibi that was busted.

SIMON. You lying little schemer,

SIMON.	AGGIE.
I had nothing to do with Daria!	It was your problem, not mine!

INSPECTOR. *Will you both please be quiet!!* You are *both* under arrest,

(We hear a siren in the distance.)

and I believe I see my men coming up the drive, *now move along!*

AGGIE. …Idiot!

*(**AGGIE** and **SIMON** leave the room, and the **INSPECTOR** starts to follow them.)*

MADGE. You were right about Aggie. What made you think of it?

GILLETTE. Just getting outside helped clear my head. And then I thought: How could Simon kill Hugo alone? Just loosening the strap on his ski? Too unpredictable. Aggie must have drugged the poor man, or perhaps they killed him together first, then staged the accident. I suppose we'll find out at the trial.

FELIX. I hadn't thought of a trial. Do you think they could beat the rap?

GILLETTE. I doubt it. But if this were a play, it would make a good sequel.…Inspector. Well done.

INSPECTOR. Thank you, William. We get our man. And girl. Whatever.

Come, you spirits
That tend on mortal thoughts, unsex me here,
And fill me from the crown to the toe top-full
Of direst cruelty!

If you need an actress, give me a jingle. I might be available.

*(The **INSPECTOR** exits, leaving **FELIX**, **MADGE** and **GIL-LETTE** onstage. There's a moment of stunned silence.)*

GILLETTE. Amazing.

MADGE. Aggie. Who would have guessed.

FELIX. Well I did, actually.

MADGE. What do you mean?

FELIX. I always thought there was something suspicious about her. She was too perfect, too…satisfied, which is why I followed her out here last night during dinner. I had a feeling she was up to something.

MADGE. I thought you were out here fooling around with Daria.

FELIX. Madge. Me?

GILLETTE. *(to* **FELIX***)* I wouldn't push it, if I were you.

(**MADGE** *and* **FELIX** *take hands.* **GILLETTE** *looks away.*)

MADGE. I'm so sorry, Willie. Were you in love with her?

GILLETTE. I think I was for a moment. But what is love? Tis not hereafter.

FELIX. Present mirth hath present laughter,

MADGE. What's to come is still unsure.

FELIX. In delay there lies no plenty,

GILLETTE. Then come kiss me, sweet and twenty,

MADGE. Youth's a stuff will not endure.

FELIX. That's all well and good, but "sweet and twenty" tried to blow your brains out.

GILLETTE. Sweet and twenty usually does.

(**FELIX** *picks up the gun.*)

Careful with that, it's loaded.

FELIX. Oh it is not.

GILLETTE. Yes it is. I emptied only the first chamber. How else to catch a master criminal?

FELIX. *(waving the gun around without even noticing it, making* **GILLETTE** *and* **MADGE** *more and more nervous)* Oh stop it. You mean to say that you emptied the first chamber of every single one of these guns?

GILLETTE. Yes!

MADGE. *(dodging the gun)* Felix! Be careful!

FELIX. *(waving the gun like a schoolteacher shaking a finger at a pupil)* Gillette, listen to me: you are *not really* Sherlock Holmes and you've got to get over this obsession of yours.

GILLETTE. *Would you be careful with that! It's loaded!*

FELIX. Oh it is not and I'll prove it!

(He raises the gun above his head and points it at the ceiling, ready to fire.)

MADGE. *Don't!*

GILLETTE. *(in a different, more serious tone)* …Wait a moment, I have a question. If Aggie and Simon didn't kill Daria, then who did?

(At which moment, **MARTHA** *bustles down the stairs in her nightgown.)*

MARTHA. Sorry, sorry, I can see you're busy, but there's something I forgot to do…Oh, what is it?…Oh yes, of course.

(She spies the knife that killed **DARIA**, *still lying on the desk where the* **INSPECTOR** *left it. She picks it up and gives it a good cleaning with her handkerchief.)*

We can't leave this just lying around, now can we? It still might have my fingerprints on it. They'd think I was crazy as a bed bug.

GILLETTE. Mother?

MARTHA. I'm sorry, dear, but I had to do it. She would have ruined you.

(She hangs the knife on the wall where it was originally.)

There. Now everything's perfect again and we can all go to bed. Merry Christmas!

(She smiles happily at her dear ones, who are all safe… and dumbfounded.)

(At this moment there is a screech of music and **DARIA**, *still alive, lurches out of nowhere onto the French door from outside. We see her plastered against the glass – while simultaneously, hand still raised,* **FELIX** *fires the gun into the ceiling, surprising even himself.)*

(BANG!)

(The final moment of the Beethoven quartet fills the air.)
(curtain)